The Wideloopers

Tod Bailey rides out of Dodge City a happy man. He has sold his herd, and the only job remaining before collecting his payment is to deliver the beef to the buyer's corrals. But these happy stakes will not last for long: tragedy strikes before he reaches his camp and Bailey is greeted with utter chaos on his arrival; his herd is stolen by rustlers, Packy Lambert is dead, and his young brother is dying with a bullet in his chest.

As he sets out to locate the rustlers and to avenge his brother, Bailey realizes he is caught up in a much larger far-reaching plot. His anger flames as he goes after his cattle and hunts his brother's killers. There can be only one victor in the fiery climax to come.

Range Grab
Bank Raid
Range Wolves
Gun Talk
Violent Trail
Lone Hand
Gunsmoke Justice
Big Trouble
Gun Peril
War at the Diamond O
Twisted Trail
Showdown at Singing
  Springs
Blood and Grass
The Hanna Gang
Raven's Feud
Hell Town
Faces in the Dust
Steel Tracks – Iron Men
Marshal Law
Arizona Showdown
Shoot-out at Owl Creek

The Long Trail
Running Crooked
Hell's Courtyard
Kill or Be Killed
Desperate Men
Ready for Trouble
Border Fury
Prairie Wolves
Gunslinger Breed
Violent Men
Colorado Clean-Up
Running Wild
Blood Trail
Guns for Gonzalez
Sudden Death
Hell-Bent
Rogue Soldiers
Gun Storm
Nebraska Shoot-Out
Ruthless Men
Black Horse Creek

The Wideloopers

Corba Sunman

A Black Horse Western

ROBERT HALE · LONDON

ISBN 978-0-7198-1618-5

Robert Hale Limited
Clerkenwell House
Clerkenwell Green
London EC1R 0HT

www.halebooks.com

Typeset by
Derek Doyle & Associates, Shaw Heath
Printed and bound in Great Britain by
CPI Antony Rowe, Chippenham and Eastbourne

ONE

Tod Bailey felt pretty good as he headed back to the herd he had brought to Dodge City, aided by his young brother Thad and old Packy Lambert. He had got a good deal from Henry Westcott, a cattle buyer in town, and did not mind the rain in his face as he rode through the night to the flats outside Dodge where they had made camp that afternoon to hold the cattle pending their sale. This was the end of the trail. When he collected the dough for the herd they would head out west to California and the new life they had planned and worked for.

He pulled his chin into his slicker and tugged the brim of his Stetson lower to shield his eyes from the pelting rain. At twenty-six years old, he was tall in the saddle – over six feet – big-boned and well-fleshed: a hard man in a tough country. His blue eyes were mere slits as he peered through the rain.

Lightning flashed through sagging clouds and a growl of thunder rattled across the range. He pushed on faster, although his herd was bunched in a draw that was barred with rough-cut poles to prevent a stampede. Bailey hunched in his saddle and shook his reins. He needed to get back to the herd.

A six-gun stabbed a long red muzzle flame through the uncertain darkness, coming from his left, and he reined aside instantly although he did not hear the sound of the shot or the passing slug. The gun spat three more ribbons of fire in his direction. He sprang out of the saddle and reached for his pistol, which was holstered on the outside of his slicker. His horse ran on into the shadows. Bailey threw himself down and was ready to fight. These attackers had to be rustlers after his herd.

A flash of lightning illuminated the darkness. He saw the black figures of two riders moving into the shadows off to his left. Muzzle flame spurted again and he returned fire instantly. Thunder clashed, and all other sounds were blotted out. He saw one figure slump in his saddle before darkness pressed in again.

He could see nothing, and looked around worriedly, aware that he was very close to his camp. He sensed that the man who had shot at him had not halted, and went for his horse, which had run on several yards.

The wind whistled in his ears as he regained his saddle and pushed on, ready for trouble, but within minutes he recognized the lay of the ground ahead and reined up to peer around. He saw the dim outline of their chuck wagon with its two-horse team knee-hobbled close by, and made out the tarpaulin shelter they had erected to keep the rain off their camp. But there was no sign of his brother Thad or old Packy. He went to the blocked draw, and halted abruptly when he saw that the poles had been withdrawn. The steers were gone! A cold shaft of fear stabbed through him.

He dismounted and walked his horse into the campsite. A corner of the tarp was flapping furiously in the wind. The small fire was out, flooded by the slashing rain. He spotted a still figure lying in the mud and went to it, fearful now, his breathing restrained. He dropped to his knees and a flash of lightning revealed the hard-bitten features of old Packy, stark in death. A dark splotch of blood on the old man's chest marked the bullet hole that had killed him.

Bailey regained his feet, desperate now, breathing shallowly through his gaping mouth, and looked around for his brother Thad. He walked around the little camp, waiting for lightning to give him illumination. He was not relieved when he found no sign of Thad, and he widened his search, his right hand resting on the butt of his pistol although he did not expect more trouble. The cattle were gone and the rustlers with them.

He failed to find Thad, and went back to the deserted camp. Thad's horse was missing, and he wondered if his brother had headed out after the thieves. The rain was easing now; the storm was passing over. Inky blackness covered the range and he could not see anything. Impatience filled him but he curbed it. He was helpless until daylight.

He attended to his horse before relighting the campfire. He covered Packy's still figure with a blanket and then cooked some bacon. He was wiping grease from his plate with a piece of bread when he heard the sound of a horse approaching from the surrounding shadows and got swiftly to his feet. He covered the direction of the approaching rider. A horse loomed up out of the night.

The horse halted and the rider tumbled out of his saddle. Something familiar about the appearance of the man sent a pang through Bailey and he ran forward, recognizing his brother Thad. He holstered his pistol – dropped to his knees beside the prone figure.

'Thad, where you been?' he demanded. 'What happened here?'

Firelight illumined his brother's pale face. Thad's eyes flickered but did not open. Bailey slid a big hand under Thad's head and raised it out of the mud. He lifted his brother's slight figure and carried it to the fire, and by the flickering light he saw blood on Thad's chest. The splotch was almost dead centre, and a harsh sigh escaped Bailey as he opened the slicker to expose the chest.

Bailey saw at a glance that the wound was fatal. He stroked Thad's upturned face, his big hand gentle.

'Thad, can you tell me what happened?' he demanded in a low tone.

The sound of his voice reached through Thad's shock and brought a reaction. The youngster opened his eyes and he looked at Bailey. His right hand came up out of the mud and grasped Bailey's arm.

'It's good to see you, Tod.' A groaning rattle sounded in the young voice. 'They took us by surprise – six of them, Packy went down from the first shot. He never had a chance. I ducked out into the shadows and took them on as they stole the herd. They were slick. The steers went like they were greased. I followed, trading lead with them, and nailed one of them before I was hit. I was lucky to get clear. All I could think of was getting back here to tell you what

8

happened. I'm sorry, but I did what I could. You left me in charge and I let you down! I'm real sorry!'

'Don't blame yourself, Thad. You did right!' Bailey gripped Thad's hand, and then he fell silent, aware that he was talking to a dead man.

He sat in a timeless void, shocked beyond comprehension and unable to think straight. The fire died to a dim red glow before he stirred and got to his feet. He broke camp, moving and acting instinctively. He placed the two bodies in the wagon, tied the spare horses to the back of the vehicle, hitched up the team and set off for Dodge City. In the morning he would return to this grim spot and look for tracks. He wanted his herd back, and he wouldn't rest until the rustlers were dead.

The rain eased and the sky cleared. Stars shone overhead and a thin crescent of the moon was shining over in the west. Bailey sat on the wagon seat as if made of stone, his thoughts stilted, submerged in shock. He could not believe that Thad and Packy were dead. Flashes of their long trip from Wain's Peak, Colorado kept appearing in his mind. He could hear Thad's cheerful voice ringing in his ears, and then saw the nightmarish vision of his brother lying dead in the mud of the campsite.

It was almost midnight when he rode into the main street of Dodge City. Lights were burning brightly and several saloons were still busy. He reined in where a sign proclaimed the sheriff's office and jumped down from the wagon. The sidewalk was busy, with anonymous figures passing to and fro, restless and pleasure-seeking.

Bailey entered the office. A middle-aged man with a law star pinned to his shirt was seated at a desk, reading a newspaper. He looked up at being disturbed, and subjected Bailey to a long, cool stare.

'I'm Buck Stanton, the deputy sheriff,' he said. 'What can I do for you, mister? You look like you found some trouble.'

Bailey told him tersely, with only half his mind on what he was saying; the rest of his brain was screaming repeatedly that Thad was dead and the herd stolen. The deputy listened with expressionless face, his eyes intent and unblinking. When Bailey fell silent Stanton cleared his throat and leaned forward slightly in his seat.

'It sounds like the work of Nick Mason's bunch,' he said.

'Before my brother died he said he nailed one of the rustles.' Bailey spoke through clenched teeth.

'I'll want to take a look at the dead rustler. If it is one of Mason's gang we'll know who to look for.'

'I'll be riding out at sunup,' Bailey said 'Where's the undertaker at?'

'Leave your wagon out front. I'll get Mack Dean to collect the bodies, and Dean will leave your wagon outside his place on the back lots. I'll have Pete McKay from the stable take care of your horses.'

'Thanks.' Bailey nodded. 'I'll see McKay. I've got three saddle horses tied to the back of the wagon.'

'OK. If you show up here in the morning at first light I'll ride out with you. I'm the only lawman in town right now. The sheriff and two deputies were killed a week ago. We got a new man coming in to boss the law department, He's arriving next week.'

Bailey turned away. He left the office, collected the

saddle horses from behind the wagon and swung into his saddle. He rode along the street to the stable. His thoughts were moving through his mind in a dark undercurrent.

He led the horses into the barn, which was dimly lit by a lantern hanging from a nail in a post. A man appeared in the doorway of a small office to the left of the main door.

'Howdy,' he greeted. He was a tall beanpole of a man, probably in his fifties. His hat was pushed back to reveal a shock of white hair. 'I'm Pete McKay. You're late getting into town.' He paused, and then came forward, peering intently. 'I saw you in here earlier, huh? I never forget a face.'

'Yeah, I was here. I'll leave these three horses here until tomorrow, and there are a couple of horses with my wagon. When the undertaker has removed two bodies from the wagon he'll bring the horses in. Take care of them, huh?'

'I sure will. Who's been killed?'

'My brother and my pard were guarding our herd just outside town while I came in to talk with a cattle buyer. When I got back to our camp the cattle had been stolen and my crew were dead.'

McKay swore under his breath and shook his head. 'There's too much of that going on around here,' he said harshly. 'You ain't the first cattleman to find trouble. You had a small herd, huh?'

'Three hundred head.'

'That's small, and I reckon you won't have to look far for the thieves. It sounds like the Mason gang. You'll be

11

going back to your camp in the morning to look for tracks, huh?'

'That's my intention.' Bailey's words were clipped. 'Can you tell me anything about the rustlers?'

McKay stepped back and raised his hands palms outwards. 'Hey, I don't know a blamed thing about what goes on around Dodge. It's safer that way. I'm sorry I can't help you. Have you been to the law office?'

'Sure! There's nothing I can do before sunup.'

'There's a lot wrong with the set-up around here, and it don't look like it'll get any better in future. If you go looking for Mason and his bunch then you'll wind up dead, like your brother. It's been tried before, and Mason is still on top of the heap. You'd best cut your losses and head on back to where you came from.'

'I'll do what I've gotta do, come hell or high water.' Bailey's harsh tone grated on the silence.

'I guessed you'd say that. I reckon you'll need a lot of luck, mister.'

'Luck ain't in my cards,' Bailey replied.

McKay went back into his office. Bailey settled the three horses in adjoining stalls and took care of them, his thoughts clamouring in the back of his mind. When he left the barn he walked along the street to the nearest saloon, paused to peer over the batwings, and then entered. He had a cold spot in his belly that needed whiskey, and he walked to the bar, his cold gaze flitting around.

Two men were drinking at the bar and five more were playing poker at two of the small tables. A big man in a grey store suit was standing behind the bar, talking to the two men, who were wet; had likely ridden through the recent storm. Bailey saw that the barkeep was holding a pocket watch in his right hand, examining it closely. He glanced up as Bailey reached the bar, but returned his gaze to the watch.

'How much do you want for it?' he asked one of the men.

'How about serving me?' Bailey cut in.

'Be with you in a minute,' the barkeep replied. He opened the front of the watch and it chimed.

Bailey heard the sound and froze. He studied the two men at the bar. They were dressed in range clothes and were hard-faced with alert eyes, and looked as if they were ready to fight at the drop of a hat. Long riders, he thought.

'I've waited too long already,' he rapped. 'Gimme a whiskey, and make it quick. I've got other things to do.'

The barkeep came along the bar, still holding the watch, collecting a glass and a bottle of whiskey on his way. He set down the glass in front of Bailey and poured a measure of whiskey into it. Bailey had eyes only for the watch. It was attached to a gold chain that had a tiny silver bell fixed to the other end. Bailey slapped a silver coin on the bar. The barkeep picked it up and, as he turned away, Bailey said:

'Before you go, take a look in the back of that watch and I'll bet I can tell you what is written there.'

'Hey,' called one of the two men at the bar. 'Bring that watch back here, barkeep.'

Bailey reached for his holstered pistol, drew it with uncanny speed, and pointed its black muzzle at the barkeep.

13

'Do like I said,' Bailey rasped.

'It ain't my watch,' the bartender said quickly. He gazed into the muzzle of the gun and his face paled perceptibly.

Bailey watched him intently, and could clearly see the two men along the bar. The one who had handed the watch to the barkeep was uneasy, and called again. He was unable to see that Bailey had drawn his gun.

'I want that watch back pronto, barkeep,' he called. 'I've changed my mind about selling.'

'I'm the one with a gun on you,' Bailey rapped at the barkeep. 'Do like I say. Open the back of the watch and I'll tell you what's written inside.'

The barkeep's fingers trembled as he opened the watch. He gazed inside it for a moment before looking up at Bailey.

Bailey's voice crackled. 'It says "Packy Lambert – his twenty-first birthday".'

'Hey, that's right,' the barkeep said. 'How'd you know that?'

Bailey was watching the two men along the bar. The one who had handed the watch to the barkeep dropped his right hand to his side and then lifted it quickly, filled with his gun. Bailey saw the muzzle swinging to cover him, flipped his pistol to the left, and fired instantly.

The crash of the shot rocked the big room and rattled the array of bottles on the back of the bar. The barkeep cowered away from Bailey, keeping his hands in sight. He froze, his face shocked, the watch clenched in his right hand. The man who had handed him the watch jerked when Bailey's slug hit him in the chest. He fell sideways against the second man, who clutched at him, and they

14

both fell to the floor.

Bailey moved to his left, gun levelled, covering both men. The man he had shot was motionless – the other scrambled to his feet and reached for his gun.

'Hold it!' Bailey rapped. His ears were protesting at the noise of the shot. He covered the man as he came upright. 'Get rid of your gun.'

The gun, half-drawn, was lifted out of it holster and dropped to the floor. The man straightened and raised his hands shoulder high. His face was tense, his eyes narrowed and filled with tension. The barkeep leaned on the bar, the watch still clutched in his right hand, his face pasty-white.

'What's this all about?' he demanded.

The batwings creaked and Bailey threw a glance to his left. Buck Stanton, the deputy sheriff, entered the saloon at a run, a gun in his hand. He came to Bailey's side, taking in the situation at a glance.

'You found someone you were looking for?' he demanded.

'It sure looks that way,' Bailey explained tersely. There was not a movement in the big room. The card-players were motionless in their seats. 'The barkeep can tell you what happened,' Bailey ended.

'What about it, Joe?' Stanton demanded.

'Sure.' The barkeep nodded vigorously. 'It was like he said. Those two jaspers came in, and one of them showed me a gold watch he wanted to sell. This man came in, and when he saw the watch he said he could tell me what was written inside it, and he sure as hell did!'

'I recognized the chime when you opened the front,'

15

Bailey said. He took the watch from the barkeep. 'It belonged to my pard, Packy Lambert, and whoever shot him this evening took it off his body.'

'One of the rustlers, I'll bet, huh?' Stanton turned to the dead man's companion, who was young, in his early twenties, lean and hardlooking, his brown eyes filled with a mean expression. 'What's your name, stranger, and where do you come from?'

'I'm Bill Tate from Nebraska way. I was putting my horse in the barn when this guy came in and we got talking. He said he'd just hit town, like me, and we came along here for a drink. I don't know him from Adam. He offered to sell that watch to the barkeep, and the next thing I know there was shooting and the guy is dead.'

'I don't believe you,' Bailey snapped. 'You were pulling your gun as you got up. I've got you pegged as a rustler.'

'Hold up there,' Stanton butted in. 'I'll handle this according to the law.' He bent, picked up Tate's gun, and kicked the gun dropped by the rustler across the wide room. 'Joe, get Mack Dean over here to take care of the stiff, and tell him I'll talk to him later. Bailey, keep your gun on Tate and we'll head for the law office after I've searched the dead man. Then we'll try to get to the bottom of this.'

Bailey held his gun on Tate, who remained motionless with his hands up. Stanton bent over the dead man and searched him, removing several items from his pockets. One of the items was a letter, and the deputy glanced at the front of it.

'This was sent to someone called Al Frazee – the dead man, I guess. OK, let's move along to the jail. We've got some talking to do.'

Stanton drew his gun and Bailey holstered his weapon. He carried Packy's watch as they left the saloon for the law office, with Tate ahead of them; their boots thudded on the sidewalk. Bailey felt ready to drop. He'd had a long day, and his grief had overwhelmed him. He was rigid with tension, and felt as if he was lost in an unreal world. The sunny future he and Thad planned had crashed and he was left in a state of uncertainty. But there was one stark thought in his mind, which reared up like a signpost. He would not rest until all the rustlers were down in the dust.

They entered the law office, and Stanton made Tate empty his pockets before searching him. Satisfied that Tate had not kept anything back, he turned his attention to Tate's belongings' and snatched up a wad of paper money.

'This is a lot of dough,' he said. 'There must be fifty dollars. Where did you get it from, Tate?'

'I trailed from Nebraska with a herd of steers that'll be reaching here in a couple of days. The trail boss sent me on ahead to scout around for him. He gave me the dough.'

'What outfit were you riding with?' Stanton demanded.

'Bat Riley's Lazy R. They'll be pulling into the yards day after tomorrow.'

Stanton thrust out his bottom lip as he considered. He nodded. 'OK, so I'll put you in a cell until the herd shows up and we'll see if someone can identify you.'

Tate protested but Stanton cut him short as he picked up a bunch of keys.

'You're wasting your breath,' he said. 'Go through that

door in the back wall and I'll lock you in a cell. I'll make some other enquiries about you while we wait for that herd you rode with to show up.'

Bailey stood motionless in the office until Stanton returned from the cells.

'That's all we can do right now,' the deputy said. 'But we have got one of the rustlers who hit your camp. Are you sure about that watch?'

'It was Packy's all right.' Bailey opened the watch and showed it to Stanton.

'So the only place Frazee could have got hold of the watch is from Lambert's body, huh? Did you see Lambert with the watch before you left your camp to come into town?'

'I saw him with it,' Bailey said harshly. 'Now all we've got to do is find the men Frazee was riding with. They've got to be around here someplace. Have you seen Frazee before? You mentioned a rustling gang when I was in here earlier.'

'Nick Mason. Yeah, he runs a gang of half a dozen cattle thieves who have been operating around here for a long time. We don't know what Mason looks like, and there's nothing on the rest of the gang. They're a slick bunch and don't make many mistakes. You dropping on Frazee is a stroke of luck, and we'll try to take advantage of it. Your stolen cattle were branded, I guess?'

'Sure. I run the BB ranch.'

'So I'll look up all the cattle buyers around here and tell them to watch out for BB steers. We might strike lucky.'

'I don't think the rustlers will be fool enough to push the steers in here. If they're as clever as you say then I'd

18

expect them to head for another market – Abilene – or they'd try to alter the brands on my steers.'

'We've got something to work on, anyhow. Are you staying in town tonight?'

Bailey glanced at the watch and nodded. 'The sun will be up in five hours. I'll bed down in the livery barn. I want to pull out before the sun shows.'

'I'd like to ride with you, but we're short-handed around here until the new sheriff shows up. The best thing you can do is try to track your herd, and if you do find any sign of the rustlers then come back to me and I'll turn out with a posse. I'd like to catch Nick Mason red-handed. He's been making a real nuisance of himself lately.'

'If I catch up with him there won't be a lot left of him for you to handle,' Bailey said through clenched teeth. He turned to the door and departed into the night. . . .

TWO

Bailey moved silently through the shadows along Main Street, his gaze missing nothing although his mind and thoughts were introspective. He was badly shocked by his brother's death. He stepped into the shadows of an alley when the batwings of the saloon were thrust open as he approached, and he stood motionless in the dark silence while an anonymous figure passed by the alley mouth. When Bailey went on again his hand was close to the butt of his holstered gun.

The livery barn was in total darkness when he reached it, and the big front door was closed and locked. He faded into nearby shadows and looked around the long street, which was now mostly unlit. The lights of the saloon went out even as he regarded them, and he suppressed a shiver as the breeze cut at him, He entered the wide alley beside the barn and made his way to the back lots, feeling his way with his left hand outstretched. He emerged from the alley and found himself beside a corral at the rear of the barn.

He slipped behind the poles and approached the barn.

A flight of exterior steps led up the rear wall to a door in the loft, which was open. As he made his way up the steps a gun blasted and a ribbon of orange muzzle flame stabbed through the shadows of the alley mouth he had just left. A bullet thudded into the woodwork beside him with a deadly tearing sound. He raced up the remaining steps and hurled himself headfirst into the loft.

Two more shots blasted. Bailey drew his gun and turned back to the stairs. The echoes of the shooting faded slowly as he watched for movement in the corral. When he saw two skulking figures entering the corral from the alley he dropped flat and remained motionless, his chin pressing against the floorboards of the loft, his gun cocked and ready for action. He lost sight of the men as they gained the shadows at the bottom of the steps, but he could hear the mutter of their harsh voices, and wondered who they were and why they were after him.

Boots scraped on the steps. Bailey cocked his pistol and waited. The sounds drew nearer and he moved back a couple of feet. Starshine softened the darkness, and there was a faint lightness in the sky where the clouds had blown away. The tall doorway was clearly visible. Bailey tensed and, when a head came into view at the top of the stairs, he swung his pistol and crashed the long barrel against the man's forehead. The man groaned and relaxed, and then went slithering and falling down the steps.

A gun blasted from below, and two bullets smacked into the doorway. Bailey inched forward again and saw the flash of the last shot. He slanted the muzzle of his gun and bracketed the area around the flash, firing four shots. He reloaded instantly while watching the corral. There was no

21

movement and heavy silence pressed in around him. He did not move, aware that he had to play a waiting game.

After what seemed a timeless period he heard sounds in the corral and eased forward to check. He saw a lone figure standing motionless in the corral and covered it with his gun. 'Declare yourself.' Bailey's voice echoed in the night.

'Buck Stanton.' The reply was instant. 'I guessed it was you, Bailey. There are a couple of dead men down here.'

'They jumped me as I came up to the loft. We traded some lead, and I was waiting for their next move.'

'Their next move will be to Boot Hill,' Stanton chuckled harshly. 'You don't have to come down if you don't want to. I just wanted you to know that I'm around. I wouldn't want to get plugged by you. There are too many bad-men around here trying to wipe out the local law without me risking my life with honest men.'

'I'll come down,' Bailey replied. 'I sure want to know who's been trying to kill me.' He got to his feet and descended to the corral. A huddled figure was sprawled at the bottom of the steps. Bailey bent over it, saw a shadowed, bearded face, and ascertained that the man was dead. Stanton came forward, bent over the body, and studied the face He straightened, shaking his head.

'I ain't seen him around here,' he declared. 'There's another one dead in the centre of the corral so let's check him out. I'm wondering if it was you they were after and, if so, how did they know it was you. To my way of thinking I reckon they are rustlers, and they must have been watching you since your herd got stolen.'

'I've got it figured like that.' Bailey nodded. 'But if they are rustlers then they're likely to be local men, so why can't you recognize them?'

Stanton laughed. 'This burg is bursting at the seams with johnny-come-latelies. We can't keep up with them. It would have been helpful if you had seen them taking your steers and could identify some of them. But you can't. So this has got to be done the hard way.'

They inspected the body in the corral and Stanton shook his head.

'I don't know this one either,' he said. 'I'll tell you what I'll do. I'll have these bodies on show in the mortuary and see if any of the locals can pin names to them. It's all we can do at moment, and I'm hoping we'll have some luck tomorrow when we visit your campsite. There'll be plenty of tracks out there, and maybe they'll lead us to the rustlers.'

'I'll be heading out at sunup,' Bailey said.

'I don't think you should sleep out here in the stable.' Stanton straightened from checking the dead inan's scant possessions. 'If there are others in town who want to shoot you then you'd be safer in my jail. You can sleep in a cell, and no one will sneak up on you.'

'Thanks,' said Bailey instantly. 'I'll take you up on that. I need to get some shut-eye. I've got a feeling the next few days will be tough.'

They walked to the law office, and Stanton showed Bailey into an empty cell. Bailey removed his gunbelt, dropped thankfully on to a bunk and closed his eyes. In spite of his thoughts he was asleep within minutes.

The sun peering through a window high up in the back

wall of the cell block brought Bailey to his senses. He looked at his surroundings and then got to his feet. He felt washed out, and his thoughts started hammering the moment his memory came back. He buckled on his gunbelt and then went through to the front office. Buck Stanton was sitting at the desk, his chin on his chest, his eyes closed. He was snoring.

Bailey kicked the leg of Stanton's chair and the deputy snorted and sat up quickly. He looked up at Bailey, and got to his feet.

'You're ready to head out, I guess,' he said. 'But I can't go with you. I'll be tied up around here all day, what with the dead men and all. Just take it easy out there. You could run into a lot of trouble. But if you learn anything then come back and tell me. Don't try to take on those rustlers all by yourself.'

'I'll have some breakfast and then get moving.' Bailey headed for the street door. 'If the rustlers are out there then I'll find them. I'll be seeing you.'

He paused to check his pistol before leaving the office. The street was already awake, with men moving about their business. He found a diner along the street and went in for breakfast, afterwards making for the livery barn. Within ten minutes he was riding out of town, steeling himself for the job in hand as he rode back to where his herd had been held the night before.

The sky was brilliant, cloudless. The ground was soft and had that well-soaked appearance. Bailey guessed he would have no trouble finding tracks, and the thought of action against the rustlers filled him with eagerness. He battled mentally with his emotions, got them under control, and was fully alert when he rode into the camp-site.

There were plenty of tracks in the soft ground. He followed the direction taken by the stolen herd, and kept his right hand close to the butt of his holstered pistol. It was quite likely that the rustlers would leave a man or two on their back trail to guard against pursuit, and he was ready for any action that might arise. He made good time because the tracks were well defined in the rain-soaked ground.

When he came across the huddled figure of a man on the ground he dismounted and checked it over. There were no means of identification on the body and nothing in its pockets. He stood thinking for a few moments. This was the rustler Thad must have shot. He left the body lying and continued, aware that the herd would not have covered many miles during the night. He pushed on faster, urged by the thought of making contact with the rustlers.

High noon found him heading north-west. The ground was drying out fast under the blazing sun, but the tracks were fresh and clear. He rode more cautiously, certain that he was getting very close to the herd, and as time passed he grew eager for action. He headed left of the tracks, making for nearby high ground, paused on a ridge, and then moved back swiftly off the skyline. A cabin, a corral and two shacks were at the bottom of the slope, and about sixty steers were grazing in the middle distance.

Bailey dismounted quickly and led his horse away from the crest. He trailed his reins and pulled his Winchester out of its saddle boot, eager for action. He dropped flat, bellied up to the crest and peered down the slope. There were four horses in the corral but no sign of men. He studied the range and, from his vantage point, could see the tracks of the rustled herd off to the right, heading into the distance.

He slid backwards, intending to get his horse and circle the herd to check the brands, but as he got to his feet he caught a glimpse of a sudden movement to his left. He swung quickly, then halted the movement. A young woman was emerging from a nearby draw, holding a shotgun, and the deadly barrels were lined up on his chest. Her expression was tense, and she looked determined enough to shoot him as she motioned with the shotgun for him to raise his hands.

'Drop that rifle,' she called. 'What are you doing snooping around here?'

Bailey dropped the rifle and raised his hands. She was tall and fair-haired, wore faded blue denim pants, a check shirt, and a flat-crowned hat. She was in her middle twenties. Her pale-blue eyes held the glitter of decision in their depths, and Bailey sensed that she would shoot him without hesitation if he made the wrong move.

'I'm not snooping around,' he replied. 'I'm following a rustled herd, saw the ranch below and I'm trying to make up my mind about dropping in. I can see the tracks of my herd going on into the distance off to the right.'

The girl's suspicion faded, but she did not relax her alertness, and the shotgun continued to cover his chest.

'I live at the ranch,' she said. 'It's my dad's place. He's Mike Pearson. I'm Stella. I didn't hear anything last night, what with the storm and all, and Dad didn't mention anything this morning. But if you're who you say you are then you're welcome to come down and speak to Dad.'

'I'm Tod Bailey,' he responded. 'My brother Thad was shot dead last night by the rustlers.'

Her expression hardened at his words and she lowered the shotgun.

'There's too much of that kind of trouble going on around here,' she mused. 'I'm sorry about your brother. When I came on you watching the ranch I thought you were one of the men who are trying to steal it from us.'

'Steal it?' Bailey echoed.

'That's right. We've been getting trouble for weeks now.'

'I'm sorry to hear that. I hope you get clear of your trouble. I've got to get on. I need to catch up with the rustlers pretty quick.'

'And what will you do if you get to them?' she demanded.

'Whatever it takes.' His tone was flat but his eyes glinted with resolution. 'It depends how many there are. I'll take it as it comes.'

'I wish you luck.' She turned away, crossed the ridge, and went striding down the slope, leaving Bailey with a vivid impression of her light-blue eyes.

He stood on the crest and watched her progress for a moment before heaving a sigh and turning to his horse. He mounted and followed her down the slope. She was moving fast, and did not look back at him although she must have heard his horse. When he reached level ground he cast a last look at her, then turned his mount to get back to the cattle tracks.

He rode resolutely, watching his surroundings alertly. The tracks crossed a regular trail that came from the Pearson ranch and headed in the direction of Dodge City. Three riders were on the trail, approaching from Dodge. Bailey reined up and sat his mount, watching them, his right hand on his thigh close to his holstered gun. He wondered if the newcomers were with the rustlers, but when they drew nearer he could see that two of them were wearing town suits. The third man was in range clothes, and Bailey's eyes narrowed when he saw twin pistols on the belts around the man's waist.

The two-gun man said something to his companions and they reined in while he came ahead towards Bailey. Intent on his business, Bailey wanted to question the new-comers about the rustled cattle. He waited stolidly for the gunman to arrive, chafing inwardly at the delay. His herd was putting distance between them, and he needed to push on, but he could not afford to miss a chance of getting information about his quarry.

The gunman came at a lope, his reins in his left hand, his right hand down by his waist. He was big-framed, hard-looking, with a rugged face and cold blue eyes. His clothes were clean, not range-stained, and Bailey doubted that he had ever handled a rope or worked on a ranch. He halted a couple of yards from where Bailey sat motionless in his saddle and leaned forward, his face taking on an aggressive expression.

'Who are you, Buster?' he demanded brusquely. 'What's your business here?'

'I'm trailing rustled cattle,' Bailey replied, ignoring the challenge in the near-insolent tone. He jerked a thumb at

28

the tracks in the soft ground. 'Have you seen any sign of them?'

'I've got better things to do than stick my nose into what don't concern me. You've come from the Pearson ranch, I reckon, so what were you doing there?'

Bailey did not reply. He did not like the question or the attitude of the big man. But he was not about to set himself against a professional gunslinger. He shook his reins, turned his horse in the direction of the tracks, and touched spurs to the animal's flanks, showing his back to the gunman.

'Hold up there,' the gunman called. 'I ain't finished with you.'

Bailey ignored the command. When he did not halt he heard the crash of a shot, and a bullet struck the ground within inches of his mount's right foreleg. He reined in, turned his horse to face the gunman, and sat motionless, gripping his reins. Anger flared through him but he kept it in check.

'All you got to do is answer a couple of questions,' the gunman said. 'You don't have to answer, but if you don't I'll put a slug in your belly.'

'I've told you what I'm doing,' Bailey said through his teeth. He jerked a thumb towards the cattle tracks. 'Those are my cattle being pushed along there, and the drovers are rustlers. They killed my brother last night when they stole the herd, and I'm anxious to catch up with them. I haven't been to the ranch back there. I passed it by. That's it, mister.'

'I'll take your word for it.' The gunman waggled his pistol slightly. 'Go on. Get to hell out of here, and keep riding.'

Bailey turned his horse and continued following the cattle tracks. He exhaled sharply through his nose, not liking the way he had knuckled under to the threat of the gun. But only a fool would set himself against a gun-slammer holding a weapon. He glanced over his shoulder and saw the three men riding on to the Pearson ranch. An image of Stella Pearson floated before his eyes and he sighed and shook his head. She had told him someone was trying to take the ranch from her father. But it was none of his business. He had enough trouble on his own plate without sticking his nose into something that did not concern him.

He glanced back once more. The trio had disappeared beyond a rise. Bailey heaved a sigh as he turned his horse in the same direction. Stella Pearson had struck him as an all-right girl and he could not ride on and leave her in trouble. He pushed his horse into a lope and headed for the ranch. When he reached a spot where he could observe the spread he saw the three men entering the yard, and a man was standing in the doorway of the cabin with a rifle in his hands. There was no sign of the girl.

Bailey rode closer, angling to remain out of sight. He saw the three men rein up before the cabin. The gunman was slightly ahead of his two companions, and appeared to be doing all the talking. The man in the doorway suddenly lifted his rifle and covered his unwanted guests, and Bailey flinched when a shot hammered and echoed across the range.

The gunman had made the fastest draw Bailey had ever seen, and the man in the doorway staggered, dropped his rifle and fell to the ground. A protest rose in Bailey's throat. Before he could act a shotgun barrel poked out of a cabin window. It blasted a single shot and a whirling load of 12-gauge pellets struck the gunman. He fell out of his saddle and raised dust when he hit the ground.

Bailey spurred his horse and drew his pistol as he went into the yard. He halted beside the two men, who were motionless in their saddles. They turned shocked faces towards him, but did not move. Bailey glanced at the gunman, who was dead, lying on his back with arms flung wide. Stella Pearson stood in the doorway of the cabin, the shotgun clasped in her hands. Her face was ashen, her eyes unblinking. She covered the two riders, but was too shocked to do more than menace them. The echoes of the shots were grumbling away.

'Point the gun someplace else,' Bailey called.

She dropped the gun and went to her father. Bailey kept his attention on the two men. 'If you're carrying guns then now would be the time to get rid of them,' he advised.

One of the men reached into a pocket and produced a small pistol. He tossed it on the ground and raised his hands.

'We didn't come here for trouble,' he said.

'Who are you, and what's your business?' Bailey demanded.

'I'm Carl Gruber and this is my associate, Frank Hayman. The dead man is Floyd Delmont. We are interested in buying this ranch from Pearson.'

'Backed up with a gun, huh?' Bailey shook his head. 'Delmont shot Pearson deliberately.'

'Delmont disobeyed orders,' Gruber said. 'There was

no need for shooting.'

Stella looked up from examining her father. 'My dad is alive!' she cried.

Bailey stepped down from his saddle, gun in hand.

'You two get down and raise your hands. Don't give me any trouble or there'll be more bloodshed.'

Both men stepped down from their mounts and raised their hands. Bailey crossed to Stella's side.

'Get your shotgun and cover those two men,' Bailey said. 'I'll look at your father.'

Tears were streaming down Stella's face. She scrambled to her feet and turned to snatch up the shotgun. When she pointed the weapon at the two men they cringed. Bailey dropped to one knee beside the wounded rancher. He looked at the bullet wound in Pearson's chest, which was high, just under the shoulder, and then looked up at the girl.

'I reckon he'll live,' he said. 'Come and take care of him. I'll handle those two.'

Stella dropped the shotgun and ran into the cabin. Bailey faced Gruber and Hayman.

'You'd better get out of here and don't come back.' He spoke curtly. 'It looks like Pearson ain't of a mind to sell. Why did you bring Delmont along? Is that the way you do business?'

Neither man replied. They turned and grabbed their reins, mounted, and swung their horses to leave.

'Hold it,' Bailey rasped. 'Take Delmont with you.'

He watched while Gruber dismounted and tried to load the corpse on the horse. When he failed he called Hayman for help. Between them, they accomplished the grim chore and then departed.

Bailey heaved a sigh as he watched them out of sight. Stella was attending to her father. Mike Pearson sat in the dust, head lolling, and Stella was bandaging his chest. The rancher was semi-conscious. Bailey drew a sharp breath as he looked at father and daughter. He knew he could not ride out and leave Stella alone. His own business would have to wait. He heaved a sigh, fought down his impatience, and went to the girl's side.

THREE

Stella's expression was bleak when she looked at Bailey. 'I'll have to take Dad into Dodge,' she said. 'He needs a doctor.'

'Gruber and Hayman are heading back that way, and if they spot you on the trail you'll probably get more trouble.' Bailey ignored the impatience gnawing at his insides, but he had already given up the idea of chasing the rustlers. This girl needed help, and he was the only one around. 'I'll ride with you, just in case.'

'But you're on the trail of those rustlers,' she protested.

'They'll keep. They won't be making more than twelve miles in a day. I'll get back on the trail when I've seen you safely to Dodge. I need to make a statement to Buck Stanton to set him right about what happened here. Gruber has the look of a shyster about him so you'll need backing up. I saw what happened. Delmont shot your father without warning, but I wouldn't put it past Gruber to say you killed Delmont in cold blood. I reckon your dad won't be able to sit a horse. Have you got a wagon?'

'There's one beside the barn. If you'll remain here with

34

Dad I'll get it ready.'

Bailey nodded. Stella got up and hurried away around the cabin. Bailey dropped to one knee beside Mike Pearson. The rancher was semi-conscious. He was lean and looked hardy – tough as leather – a man in his early fifties. His chin was on his chest and his face was ashen.

'You'll be OK,' Bailey encouraged. 'We're gonna take you into Dodge to the doctor. Just take it easy.'

Pearson groaned and shook his head. He slumped back and remained motionless in the dust, his eyes flickering. Bailey arose and paced to and fro until Stella brought the wagon into the yard. She looked as if she was in the last stages of despair. Bailey felt sorry for her. She was in bad trouble. He looked around critically. The ranch wasn't much, and he wondered why Gruber was dead set on buying it.

'I've put some straw in the back of the wagon to make it more comfortable,' said Stella as she jumped down from the seat.

Bailey picked up Pearson and carried him to the rear of the wagon. Stella climbed into the back, and Bailey placed the rancher on the straw.

'You'd better stay in the back with him,' he advised. 'I'll tie my horse at back here and drive the wagon. Is there anything you need before we set out?'

'I'd better take some water along, and I'll need some money. I'll lock up here. I shan't be coming back until I know Dad will be OK.'

She hurried into the house. Bailey tethered his horse to the back of the wagon and climbed into the driving seat. Stella came out of the house in a hurry. She was carrying a

35

large canteen, which gurgled as she threw it into the back of the wagon, and set down a covered basket on the straw. She went to collect her shotgun, put it into the wagon, and grimaced when she caught Bailey's eye. He nodded his approval. When she was settled in the wagon Bailey cracked the whip and they started for town.

He was alert as they travelled to Dodge. But he saw no sign of Gruber and Hayman. Two hours later they pulled into the main street, and Stella directed him to the doctor's house. Bailey stood by the wagon, looking around the street while Stella hurried to alert the doctor. He saw two horses tethered outside the law office, and recognized the animal Gruber had ridden.

Stella emerged from the house, followed by a tall young man carrying a medical bag. He sprang into the back of the wagon and bent over the rancher, then jumped out again almost immediately and handed his bag to Stella.

'Help me get him into my office,' said the doctor to Bailey.

They lifted Pearson out of the wagon and carried him gently into the house, where they stretched him out on an examination couch.

'Do you think he'll pull through?' Stella asked as she handed over the doctor's bag.

'He's got a good chance,' was the confident reply. 'The wound is high enough to have missed the lung. Why don't you leave me to it and come back in about two hours? I'll have a better idea of his chances by then.'

'We have to talk to the law,' Bailey said.

'I'm Marcus Alwyn, MD.'

'I'm Tod Bailey.'

Stella kissed her father's forehead before they left, and Bailey felt a pang of sympathy for her as they departed. He untied his horse from the wagon and led it across the street when they went to the law office. He noted that Gruber and Hayman had gone, and tied his mount to the hitch rail out front.

Buck Stanton was seated at his desk when they walked into the office. The deputy nodded as he looked at Bailey.

'I had a feeling you'd be showing up pretty soon,' he said. 'I've had a report of trouble out at the Pearson spread from a couple called Gruber and Hayman, and recognized you from their description of the man at the scene.' He turned his attention to Stella, 'Sit down, miss. Is your father badly hurt?'

'I don't know yet,' she replied. 'The doctor needs to examine him.'

'The report I got was that you shot and killed a man called Delmont, who was hired as a bodyguard by Carl Gruber, who runs the land agency in town. Would you tell me exactly what happened when your father was shot?'

'We'd been pestered by Gruber before, and Dad told him not to call again. When they turned up this morning Delmont shot my dad without warning, and I shot Delmont.'

'Did your father make any attempt to use force?' Stanton asked.

Stella shook her head. 'He didn't. He saw them coming, and took a rifle when he confronted them. He told me to stand at the window with the shotgun to cover him, and I was not to fire unless my life was in danger.'

'So you thought Delmont was going to shoot you after

he'd shot your father?'

'He shot Dad without warning, and, yes, I thought he would shoot me also.'

'Did he threaten you before you shot him?'

'He didn't get the chance. When he shot my dad I fired instinctively.'

'I was there,' Bailey said. 'I saw what happened, and it was exactly as Stella says.'

'I'll need a statement from each of you,' Stanton said. 'You'd better stick around town for a few days, Stella.'

'I shan't be leaving while Dad is here,' she replied.

'Where will you be staying?'

'I'll be at the general store with Mae Clarke. I usually stay with her when I'm in town.'

'OK. I don't think you need to worry about the shooting. There'll be an inquest, which you'll have to attend, but if Bailey's statement fits in with yours then there'll be no charges made over the killing.' He turned his attention to Bailey. 'How did you manage to get involved in this? I thought you were out hunting rustlers.'

Bailey explained, and Stanton nodded. 'Both of you can drop back later and make your statements. I hope your father will recover quickly from the shooting, miss.'

Stella sighed when they emerged from the office. 'I thought I would have been put in jail for what happened,' she declared.

'Not with my statement backing yours,' Bailey replied. 'I'll see you safely to the store, if that's where you'll be staying. I need to get back on the trail of my herd.'

'I'm sorry you got caught up in our trouble,' she said.

'Think nothing of it. I could see you were in big trouble

back there and I couldn't turn a blind eye to Gruber and his pards. I'm glad now that I left my trail to follow them to your place.'

He led his horse along the street, tethered it in front of the store, and they entered the building. Stella talked to a tall young woman who was serving behind the counter. Mae Clark was in her twenties; dark-haired, and had friendly brown eyes. She was attired in a white linen apron over a blue dress, and greeted Stella with great friendliness. Her expression changed when she learned that Mike Pearson had been shot, and she called to her father, who emerged from the back of the store.

'I'm glad to know you, Bailey,' said Bill Clarke when he was introduced. 'So it was you who lost the herd yesterday! I heard about it, and I reckon Nick Mason's gang did it. Sounds like his style.'

'I'll catch the rustlers,' Bailey asserted. 'I'm on their trail. I'd better take a box of .45 shells and a box of Winchester .44.40s.'

'I wish you luck.' Clarke reached for the boxes of ammunition. 'There's been a lot of trouble around here lately. Last week the sheriff and a couple of deputies were killed chasing bank robbers. Take care out there or someone will be toting you in filled with lead.'

Bailey nodded. He turned his attention to Stella, who was watching him intently.

'Thank you for helping me,' she said.

'It was my pleasure,' he replied. 'I'll drop by when I get back and see how you're making out. Take care. I'll see you around.'

He departed and put his purchases in a saddle-bag. He

mounted and paused to glance around the street. He saw Gruber and Hayman standing outside an office just along the street and recognized the man they were talking to – Henry Westcott, the cattle buyer who had agreed to buy his herd. Bailey's expression hardened. He began to turn his horse away to ride out, then he changed his mind and rode along the street to halt beside the cattle buyer. Westcott glanced at him, then took his leave of Gruber and came to Bailey's side.

'I'm right sorry to hear about your trouble,' Westcott said. He was big, broad and grim-faced; his dark eyes filled with anger. 'It's a pity you couldn't have gotten your herd into my cattle pens last night. As it is, you're the loser and I'm out three hundred head that I sorely need. I heard you'd gone out this morning to track the rustlers. Did you find them?'

'I haven't caught up with them yet,' Bailey replied, 'but I will.'

'Come and see me if you get the steers back. Our deal still stands.' He lifted a hand to Bailey and turned away.

Bailey was tense inside as he went on along the street. He glanced over his shoulder and saw Westcott entering the office into which Gruber and Hayman had gone. A painted sign was over the front window – GRUBER & HAYMAN. LAND OFFICE. He had no doubt that Gruber was crooked, riding around as he did with a tough gunhand to back him.

When he reached the end of the street he gazed over the many cattle pens surrounding the railroad tracks, and saw Westcott's name over a large barnlike building. He rode on out of town and headed back to where he had left

the tracks of the rustlers. It was the middle of the afternoon when he picked up the trail again, and he went
forward determinedly.

The ground had dried out since the storm, and in
places the tracks were more difficult to follow. After four
miles he halted and gazed at the ground to puzzle over the
fact that at least half his herd had forked to the right and
he was suddenly faced with two trails. The turn-off trail
seemed to be heading in the direction of Dodge City, and
Bailey's eyes were bleak as he considered. He decided to
follow the original trail and went on.

The sun was low in the western half of the sky when he
topped a ridge and saw a large ranch headquarters ahead.
He rode back off the skyline, dismounted, and dropped
flat to crawl forward and observe the clustered buildings.
He noted that the tracks he had been following went down
towards the ranch, and his breathing quickened as he considered that he was getting close to the rustlers. He could
see a small herd of steers grazing out beyond the big ranch
house. Shadows were spreading across the range as the
sun dipped down to the horizon.

He decided to check on the steers before deciding on
his course of action. If any of those steers bore the BB
brand then he would know what to do. He decided to wait
for full dark before going on, and led his horse back to
better cover, trying to relax as he waited.

The first stars of the evening were glinting overhead
when he decided it was time to move. He tightened his
cinch and swung into the saddle. The range was dark now,
and lights shone brightly from the ranch. He rode in a
wide circle to bypass the ranch, using low ground to mask

his movements. With the ranch behind him he eased to his left and made for the herd he had seen. He watched for movement, thinking that the rustlers would be close by, watching the herd. His grief had swamped his natural feelings and he was obsessed with getting to grips with the men who were responsible for his brother's death.

He was close to the herd, which had bedded down for the night, when he suddenly saw a campfire near by, in a depression in the ground. He reined in quickly and sat motionless, holding his horse on a tight rein while he studied the set-up. The fire was out of sight of the ranch house, and he wondered why nighthawks watching the herd would make camp with the ranch so close – unless these men were not connected to this range.

Two men were by the fire, and looked to be settled down for the night. He moved away silently and approached the herd. Starshine and a crescent moon gave some light to the range. He did not want to startle the cattle, and shook out his rope when he spotted an animal standing some way off from the herd. He cast his loop unerringly, and his mount braced itself as the steer was caught and tried to get away. Bailey dragged the animal away from the other steers and vacated his saddle, leaving his horse to keep the rope tight while he went hand over hand along it to the steer. It took him only a moment to feel for the brand, and his teeth clicked together when he identified the Double B of his brand.

He went back to his horse, shook his loop loose and set the steer free. It returned to the herd as he rode back to the campfire, wondering why his herd had been split into halves and where the other half had been taken. He was determined to get the answers to the questions looming large his mind, and ground hobbled his horse at a short distance from the camp. He drew his pistol as he walked in the rest of the way.

When he looked down into the depression he saw that one of the men was seated by the fire, eating. The other was stretched out on his blankets, apparently asleep. Bailey cocked his pistol, entered the depression, and walked silently to the fire. The seated man looked up, dropped his plate and reached for his holstered gun.

'Freeze!' said Bailey sharply.

All movement ceased. The man raised his hands instantly and sat motionless. The second man was snoring softly.

'Throw your gun away,' Bailey ordered, 'and be careful how you handle it. I'm hair-triggered.'

'Who in hell are you?' the man demanded as he disarmed himself.

'We'll get down to business in a moment,' Bailey replied. 'Down on your belly and put your hands above your head. Make a wrong move and you're dead.'

The man obeyed instantly. Bailey walked around him and kicked the foot of the sleeping man, who snorted and came awake.

'What the hell is going on, Cates?' he demanded. 'Why'd you wake me?'

'I'm not Cates,' Bailey said. 'Get up slowly and don't try anything or you'll be eating breakfast in Hell come morning. What's your name?'

'Jed Kettle. Who are you?'

'Shut your mouth. If you're carrying any weapons then

43

get rid of them now.'

There was no vocal response from Kettle. He stood up and raised his hands.

'Sit down on the other side of the fire,' Bailey said. 'Join him, Cates, if that's your name.'

'Are you a lawman?' Cates demanded when he was sitting beside Kettle.

'I'm Tod Bailey, a cattleman. My herd was stolen last night from the holding ground outside Dodge. My brother was killed – murdered by the rustlers. Those cows over there are a part of my stolen herd. Tell me what happened. I reckon you two are rustlers.'

'We ain't rustlers,' Cates said. 'We work for Carl Gruber, who runs the land agency in Dodge, and that's his ranch back there.'

Bailey digested the information, and some of the mystery enveloping him faded. He said: 'How come you're herding rustled stock on Gruber's range? Why was my herd split up back along the trail, and where's the other half gone? It looked to me like it was heading into Dodge.'

'Why ask us?' Cates retorted. 'We were told to come out here and watch those steers, and that's what we're doing. If you wanta know more you'll have to ride into the ranch and talk to Chick Raker, Gruber's foreman. He gives the orders around here, and he doesn't tell us what's going on.'

'And where is the other half of my herd going?'

'We don't know. What you see here is all we've seen. We'll ride into the ranch with you, if you like, and you can talk to Raker.'

'Sure, and I'll stick my head in your fire if you tell me

44

to.' Bailey laughed harshly. 'I'll get around to talking to Gruber and his foreman when I'm good and ready. I'm gonna take you two into Dodge and hand you over to the law.'

Both men protested, and Bailey shouted them down.

'You've got stolen cattle here,' he rapped, 'and my brother was shot dead when they were stolen from him. Save your breath for the law. You've got some questions to answer. Saddle up your horses and we'll get moving. Keep silent, and don't try anything.'

Horses were saddled and, when the two men had mounted, Bailey knotted their reins together. He tied the hands of both men, and led their horses when he set out for Dodge City. His thoughts worked over the information he had gained. He was surprised to learn that Gruber owned the ranch back there, and wondered why the land agent had been trying to get his hands on the Pearson place.

He gave up trying to find answers to the questions teeming in his mind and settled down for the ride into Dodge. It was late evening when he finally topped a rise and saw a cluster of lights in the distance. He glanced at his prisoners. They were silent, tight-lipped, and he felt no pity for them.

Main Street was shadowy with only a few lamps shining from various windows. The saloons were doing a good trade: batwings swinging incessantly, sounds battering the surrounding silence – voices calling and shouting, a tinny piano beating out tunes of the old West. Bailey straightened in his saddle and headed for the law office. He stepped down from his saddle and untied his prisoners; he drew his gun and menaced them as they crossed the side-walk. They entered the building, and Bailey followed closely.

He was pleased to see Buck Stanton seated at his desk. The deputy got to his feet when he saw the two prisoners, and grinned when he recognized Bailey at their backs. He picked up his bunch of cell keys.

'You ain't wasting any time,' he remarked. 'Are these two of the rustlers?'

'I came across them herding half my rustled stock on Gruber's range. Do you know them?'

'Yeah, they're Rafe Cates and Jed Kettle.' Stanton nodded. 'I've seen them around. So what's the story, Cates? What were you doing with rustled steers?'

'We didn't steal 'em,' Cates said. 'We work for Gruber, and this afternoon the foreman, Chick Raker, told us to keep an eye on the steers. That's all we know about them. If you wanta know more then go ask Raker.'

'OK, so I'll put you behind bars until I've had a word with Raker. Empty your pockets on the desk.'

Bailey remained silent until Stanton had locked the two protesting prisoners in a cell. When the deputy emerged from the cell block he dropped the bunch of cell keys on a corner of the desk and sat down.

'I reckon Gruber must know something about the rustling,' Bailey ventured, 'especially after the shooting out at the Pearson place. What do you know about the land agency business? Why would Gruber take a gunman along with him to conduct his business? Delmont was an out and out bully, and he shot Pearson without giving him a chance.'

46

'I'll be asking Gruber some mighty serious questions about the way he's running his business,' Stanton said. 'I've had reports about him riding roughshod around the range. There ain't any smoke without fire. So it looks like we've got a big game going on around here. I sure want to get it licked before the new sheriff shows up. Say, why don't you put on a deputy badge and work with me? I reckon we could nail this down before it gets right out of hand.'

'Do you think it ain't out of hand now?' Bailey demanded. 'My brother and my old friend Packy Lambert were killed last night. Has Tate talked yet about how he got hold of Packy's watch?'

'I've questioned him some since you were here last, but he's tight-lipped about that. I'll let him sweat a little for a couple of days, and then he might begin to open up.'

'I'd get him to say something inside of ten minutes,' Bailey said, his teeth clenched.

Stanton shook his head. 'I got to work inside the law,' he said, 'much as I'd like to go along with you. Why don't you do like I say and join me?'

'I'll think about it, but right now I've got some suspicions in my mind that I need to drag out and act on. I can't forget how Delmont shot down Mike Pearson without warning. It tells me a lot about how Gruber is operating. I've found half my missing herd on Gruber's range, and he's sure got a lot of explaining to do. I'll attend to that right now, and we'll talk about my future later.'

'Don't act against the law,' Stanton warned.

'I know my way around the law,' Bailey said in a bleak

47

tone. 'I wore a law badge for six years while saving up enough dough to start my herd. I know how many beans make five.'

'All the more reason you should work with me,' Stanton countered.

'I'll be back a little later.' Bailey turned to the door and departed.

He rode to the stable and took care of his horse. When he left the livery barn he paused for a moment and looked along the street, his eyes glinting in the reflected light of the lamps. Somewhere in this community were the men who had stolen his herd and killed his brother and old Packy and he would not rest until he had caught up with them. . . .

FOUR

Bailey traversed the street on foot until he came to the land agency building, which was squashed between a dress shop and a gun shop. The place was in darkness, but there was a light at a window on the second floor. He had passed the place during daylight, when he saw Henry Westcott talking to Gruber and Hayman, and had noticed a flight of stairs in the alley at the side of the building, which gave access to thc upper floor. He entered the alley and felt his way along through dense shadows until he reached the stairs.

He loosened his pistol in its holster as he ascended the stairs, and knocked on the door. He waited a moment, and when there was no reply he rapped the woodwork with the butt of his gun. After a few moments a man's voice called:

'Who's there?'

'Open the door. I need to talk to you,' Bailey replied.

'Come to my office in the morning after nine.'

'This won't wait. I need to talk to you about the cattle herd that was rustled yesterday. Two of the men from your ranch are in jail for stealing it.'

The sound of a bolt being withdrawn came through the door, and Bailey stiffened. He meant to handle Gruber severely and, when the door swung open and Gruber stepped into the doorway, he pushed forward, crowded Gruber back into the apartment and followed up closely. Gruber darted back out of arm's length and turned, at bay, his face expressing fear. He was gasping for breath.

'What do you want?' he demanded. 'You can't come busting in here. What did you say about two of my men being arrested?'

'Cates and Kettle. They were herding some of my stolen cattle on your range, close to your ranch house. I brought them into town and they're in jail. They've got some awkward questions to answer, and so have you.'

'I don't know anything about your stolen cattle, and if some of them are on my grass then you'd better talk to the men who drove them there.'

'You'll have to do better than that,' Bailey responded. 'My brother was killed by the rustlers, and I'm gonna get them if it's the last thing I do.'

'The man you need to talk to is Nick Mason. He runs a rustler gang around here.'

'I've heard about him. Where does he hang out when he's not stealing cows?'

Gruber's fleshy face was pale. His eyes showed fear. He was sweating, and looked uncomfortable. Bailey stepped in close and Gruber cringed.

'I mean to get some answers from you,' Bailey said, 'and I don't much care how I go about it. I aim to kill everyone who had anything to do with my brother's death, and I ain't leaving here until I get what I want. So if you know what's good for you then you'll tell me what you know.'

'What makes you think I know anything about the rustling?'

'You're playing a crooked game on this range, chasing up ranchers and making them sell out. Delmont was gonna kill Mike Pearson for no reason at all, and don't try to deny it because I was there and saw what happened. A lawful business ain't handled by a gun man, and Delmont was a real tough killer. And I found some of my herd settled down on your grass, and two of your men herding them. When they talk, and they will, I reckon you'll have to account for what's happened. So let's get down to business. Start telling me what's going on around here and if I don't like your answers I'll knock the truth out of you.'

'You won't get anywhere by throwing your weight around,' Gruber said. 'There are some tough men in town that can't be pushed. The best thing you can do is go back to where you came from and forget what happened here.'

Bailey clenched his right hand into a fist and threw a jolting punch at Gruber's jaw. The contact made a sickening sound, like a meat cleaver striking beef. Gruber dropped to the floor instantly and lay in a heap, groaning and gasping. Bailey bent over him, grasped him by the shoulders, and dragged him upright.

'Don't hit me again,' Gruber moaned. 'I don't know anything. I'm not mixed up in anything.'

Bailey hit him again, and let him fall to the floor. 'You better talk,' he rasped. 'I'll get the truth out of you before I'm through if I have to batter you all night, so save yourself a lot of pain. Get up and start talking.'

Gruber made an attempt to get up but flopped back

and closed his eyes. Bailey lifted him, and then pushed him into a chair. Blood was dribbling from Gruber's nose. He held a hand to his head and groaned.

'It can only get worse,' Bailey told him. 'Give me some names. You're a local man and you know what's going on behind the scenes. How come some of my steers were herded on to your range? Did you buy them from the rustlers?'

'I don't deal in rustled stock. I'm not in that business.' Gruber made an effort to get into an upright position.

Bailey watched him for some moments, and when he decided that Gruber was not going to talk he dealt him a blow to his left eye. Gruber fell sideways off the chair, a yell escaping him. Bailey stepped forward a half-pace and kicked sharply at the man's quivering body. Gruber yelped like a dog and got to his hands and knees. Blood trickled from his face. He gasped for breath.

'Start coming up with some names,' Bailey said. 'I'm getting mighty impatient. The men who killed my brother are still breathing God's good air, and I want to put them under.'

'There's a man in town they say is connected with the local rustlers,' Gruber gasped. 'His name is Harper Moss. He's got a saddlery along the street on the other side of the Half Chance saloon and he mixes with a tough crowd – drinking, gambling, and causing disturbances around the town. He's been jailed a couple of times for assault. If anyone knows what's going on around here then he's the man. I can't tell you anything, so you're wasting your time with me.'

'I need more than that to go on.' Bailey dragged

Gruber to his feet and held him upright. He raised his right fist and Gruber cringed. Bailey picked his spot and crashed his fist against Gruber's nose. Blood spurted, and Gruber yelled in agony. Bailey released him, and Gruber staggered backwards until he fetched up against a door. He slid sideways and fell to the floor, both hands to his face, whimpering like a kicked dog.

'My patience is running out,' Bailey declared. He bent to gasp Gruber again. 'I can keep this up all night, but can you take it? I know you're crooked, Gruber, because some of my cows were found on your range with two of your riders herding them. So you're gonna tell me all about that, and if you're lucky you may still be breathing at the end of it.'

'Don't hit me again.' Gruba gasped. 'I can't take any more. I heard that Nick Mason stole your cows, and he's holed up in a line shack on my northern line. He's got half a dozen men with him.'

'That's better.' Bailey smiled grimly. 'There's a man called Tate in jail right now, and I know for a fact that he's one of the rustlers. So tell me about him.'

'Tate is one of Mason's gang. Go after them and leave me alone.'

'I'll do that right now, but I'll be back if l get word that you are mixed up in the stealing – you can count on that.'

Bailey departed, leaving Gruber quivering on the floor. He went back to the law office, and Stanton looked up eagerly. Bailey told him what Gruber had said. Bailey picked up his cell keys and fetched Tate out of the cells. The rustler sat down on the chair placed before the desk and Bailey stood behind him. Stanton sat down opposite and motioned to Bailey.

'It's your show,' he said. 'Make him talk.'

Tate twisted in his seat and looked up at Bailey, his gaze showing apprehension. Bailey grinned, his eyes hard and cold.

'It's time you told me about the watch,' Bailey said.

'I didn't have the watch,' Tate replied, 'and I wasn't with the man who had it.'

'Start with the truth and stick to it,' Bailey warned. 'We know you're one of Nick Mason's rustlers, so open up and spill the beans.'

'Where did you hear that about me?' Tate demanded truculently.

'Gruber talked when I put some pressure on him. He told me about a man called Harper Moss, and I'm gonna call on him after I've finished with you.'

'I was gonna tell you about Moss,' Stanton cut in. 'He's a bad'un. I'll go with you when you call on him. I've waited a long time to hang something on Moss. I'll put Tate back in a cell and we'll hunt up Moss now.'

Bailey nodded. Tate was returned to his cell and Stanton made ready to leave. He locked the office door and paused on the sidewalk.

'I reckon I know where Moss will be at this time of the night,' he mused. 'Come on. With any luck we'll catch him on the hop.'

Stanton left the main street and headed through a maze of shacks and cabins built on the back lots. He knocked at a cabin door, and after a short pause a woman answered. She peered intently at them, for they were in deep shadow, and when she began to speak Stanton stepped forward, placed a hand over her mouth, and spoke hoarsely to her.

'Keep it quiet, Lola. If Moss is with you we'd like to get the drop on him, so just nod or shake your head when I ask the question. Is he here?'

She nodded instantly. Stanton drew his gun and pushed her back into the cabin, still holding her. Bailey followed and they entered the building. A man was seated at a table, eating supper, and he sprang to his feet at their entrance, dropping his hand to the butt of his holstered gun. He was tall and heavily built, wide-shouldered and muscular. Stanton stepped around Lola and lunged towards Moss, who immediately pulled his gun. Stanton struck with his pistol, caught Moss's gun hand, and the big man lost his grip on his weapon, yelled in pain, and grasped his bruised wrist.

'What the hell do you want, Stanton?' he snarled, his face screwed up with hatred.

'Just a friendly talk,' the deputy replied. 'So let's keep it that way.'

'Are you arresting me?'

'Is there any reason why I should? But then I shouldn't ask that question. There's always something I ought to arrest you for. Sit down and finish your supper while we talk.'

'The sight of you has killed my appetite.' Moss sat down and resumed his meal. 'What's on your mind? Whatever it is, I didn't do it.' He gazed at the silent Bailey. 'Who in hell are you?' he demanded.

'He lost a herd of cattle yesterday,' Stanton said, 'and his brother was killed by the rustlers.'

'So that's what this is about, huh? Yeah, I heard about it. And you think I had something to do with it?'

'If you did then you're standing on the brink of Hell as of now,' Bailey observed.

Moss gazed at him, his face expressionless. Then he nodded.

'I don't know anything about it,' he growled. 'I was working all day yesterday with Frank Aldred, the carpenter. We were out at Bar 25, putting an extension on the kitchen. Check with Aldred if you don't believe me.'

'I'll check every word,' Stanton said. 'Do you see much of Nick Mason these days?'

'I ain't set eyes on him since he took to rustling, I don't mix with bad-men.'

'Tell me what you know about Carl Gruber's business,' Stanton continued.

'What makes you think I would know anything about him?' Moss chuckled harshly. 'Have you been listening to gossip, Stanton?' He laughed again.

'This is a serious business,' Stanton reproved.

'Yeah, sure.' Moss glanced at Bailey. 'I did hear word that Mason is holed up north of here – some line shack on the range. I also heard that he's tied in with a bigger outfit that is planning to steal the range blind. And it looks like they made a start with your herd.' He glanced at Bailey again.

'Is there anything else you can tell me?' Stanton demanded.

'Nope. But I'll keep my ears open and I'll let you know if I hear anything.'

'I'll come back to you later,' Stanton said. 'You'd better

56

keep your nose clean, Moss. There's big trouble coming
for the bad-men around here.'

They departed, and Stanton grasped Bailey's arm and
pulled him into the dense shadows at the side of the cabin.

'We'll wait a few minutes.' Stanton spoke in an under-
tone. 'Maybe we've lit a fire under Moss. He's as crooked
as they come, and if he's linked to any of this present
trouble then he'll come out of the cabin at a run to warn
his pards.'

Bailey took a fresh grip on his patience and heaved a
sigh. Silent minutes passed before the cabin door opened
and Moss emerged hurriedly.

'I'll be back in about an hour,' Moss said to Lola. 'I've
got to see a couple of guys and warn them about that
deputy.'

He strode off in the direction of the main street, and
Bailey followed Stanton as he set out on Moss's heels. Moss
went to the big saloon and shouldered through the
batwings. Stanton and Dailey looked through a front
window. Moss went to the bar and spoke to a bartender,
who glanced around the big room and then jerked a
thumb towards the back of the saloon. Moss crossed to a
rear door, jerked it open, and entered a private room.

'Come on,' Stanton said. 'Let's go round the back.'

He hurried to an alley at the side of the saloon. Bailey
followed closely, and they plunged into deep shadows as
they left the main street. They gained the rear of the
saloon, and a lighted window attracted Stanton. Bailey
peered over Stanton's shoulder and looked into a room
that was furnished as an office. Moss was inside, standing
before a large desk. A big man, well fleshed and smartly

dressed, was seated at the desk. He was middle-aged, his hair long and greying. A cigar was stuck in a corner of his mouth and he was regarding Moss through a haze of blue smoke. Moss was talking but the sound of his voice could not be heard.

Stanton eased back from the window. He looked into Bailey's face, his expression showing eagerness.

'I sure wish I could hear what those two are saying,' he said.

'Let's walk in on them and make them talk,' Bailey suggested.

Stanton shook his head. 'I have to do this according to the law. Let's wait and see what comes up.'

They stood motionless in the shadows, and Bailey's patience was sorely tried. He wanted to get at the men who had killed his brother. They deserved no mercy, and he needed to see them through gun smoke. Inside the office Moss sat down beside the desk and had a drink, the urgency leaving him with the passing of a message. Then he arose and departed, looking well satisfied, and a moment later the bartender entered the office and received instructions.

'Come on,' Stanton said sharply. 'I guess Hooton is telling the 'tender to send someone to pass on Moss's message. Let's get back to the front window and see who leaves.'

They hurried back along the alley and were peering once more into the saloon when the 'tender appeared from the office. 'The man in the office is Ames Hooton, who owns the saloon,' Stanton said. 'I've had suspicions about him for a long time, considering the riff-raff hanging around this joint.'

The bartender paused at a gaming table and bent to whisper in the ear of a man sitting in a game of poker. The man, short and range-dressed, tugged his Stetson lower over his eyes, arose, and went into the office while the 'tender resumed his place behind the bar.

'The man who went into the office is Jack Attree, a layabout in town who doesn't work but always has money,' Stanton said. 'I've been watching him, but he never steps out of line. If he is mixed up with the rustlers we'll get something on him now. I feel that a big clean-up is coming.'

Several minutes elapsed before Attree emerged from the office. He went back to the table where he had been playing cards and spoke tersely to the other players. Then he came to the batwings and appeared on the sidewalk; he paused to look around the street. Stanton spoke casually to Bailey while they waited for Attree's next move. The man turned away from them and walked swiftly along the sidewalk.

'It looks like he's heading for the livery barn,' Stanton said. 'If he's gonna ride out to contact the rustlers then you can follow him and see where he goes. Will you do that?'

'Leave him to me.' Bailey nodded. 'I'll saddle my horse. You'd better not let him see you. He won't know me. I'll trail him if it takes all night.'

'Just watch his movements,' Stanton said. 'See me tomorrow at the law office. I'd do this myself but I can't leave town right now.'

Bailey nodded and went to the stable. He saw Attree

enter, and followed closely to saddle his horse. Attree led his horse outside and Bailey followed a moment later. Attree rode out of town. Bailey gave him several moments and then rode in the same direction. He rode openly, and a few minutes later a voice called to him from the shadows ahead.

'Pull up your horse and raise your hands. I've got you covered.'

Bailey obeyed and a rider came out of the shadows, a levelled gun in his right hand. Bailey recognized Attree.

'You left town on my heels,' Attree said. 'Are you following me?'

'Following you? The hell I am! I'm riding out to Gruber's ranch. Got the offer of a riding job. Have to see Gruber's foreman – what's his name? Yeah, Chick Raker. So where are you heading, and why are you so skittish? This is free range, ain't it?'

'A man can't be too careful these days,' Attree said. 'I'm going past Gruber's spread. You can ride with me as far as there.'

Bailey lowered his arms, took up his reins, and they continued along the trail. Attree did not speak until, much later, they spotted the lamps of the ranch showing as pools of yellow radiance in the dense shadows of the range.

'That's Gruber's place,' Attree said, 'I'm heading north. See you around.'

He went on. Bailey rode into the shadows and then changed direction and followed Attree. Starshine gave ghostly illumination to the range. Bailey rode carefully, keeping his quarry just within sight. Attree went on, heading north, apparently satisfied that Bailey had stopped off at Gruber's ranch. Bailey managed to ease to the left of Attree's trail, and they crossed the range at a mile-eating lope.

Some two hours passed before Bailey spotted a light ahead. He halted, dismounted, and watched Attree ride up to a lone cabin. A door was opened and a shaft of yellow light flashed across the range. Bailey moved around until he was behind the cabin, and then left his horse standing with trailing reins well out of earshot of the little building. He walked towards the shack and paused when he was beside the back wall.

A small glassless window gave a view of the area behind the cabin, and bright yellow light issuing from inside cut through the dense shadows. Bailey eased to one side of the window, removed his Stetson and peered into the single room of the shack. It was sparsely furnished: a double bunk, a small table, two chairs, and a cupboard nailed to the wall beside the door. Bailey looked around quickly before easing back, and saw Attree sitting at the table opposite a big man who was heavily built. He looked to be in his middle thirties, wearing dirty range clothes. His hat was on a corner of the table. The bright lamplight was not kind to his face. He was fleshy, his skin blotched, and his narrowed eyes were deep under his dark brows. His hair was black, matted and unwashed. He wore a cartridge belt around his waist containing a .45 pistol that was well maintained.

'So what brings you out this way, Attree? Is something wrong in Dodge?'

'Hooton paid me to ride out to tell you Bill Tate is behind bars. The guy who owned that herd you stole in the storm is in town. Mason, you killed his brother during the raid but missed him, and he's raising hell looking for you. The word is that your gang stole the steers, and you better do something before the whole deal blows up in your face.'

Bailey peered through the window again, and studied Mason's face. So this was the boss of the rustling gang. He fought against the urge to pull his gun and blast Mason clear into Hell. Common sense prevailed and he forced himself to remain motionless. His time would come.

'I get blamed for every steer stolen off this range,' Mason said. 'But I'm not the only rustler in the county. There are bigger gangs operating.'

'But you did grab that BB herd, huh?' Attree demanded.

'Sure. And we're gonna pick up another herd tomorrow night. When you go back to town you can drop a message to Gruber and he'll pass the word to the man at the top. Tell Gruber I want to know sooner about the herds coming to Dodge. I didn't hear about the BB outfit until it was almost too late, and that was why there was shooting. I don't like to kill cowboys. There's always a big ruckus about it afterwards. So I want the news sooner. You got that?'

'Sure. I'll tell Gruber. Who is the big man, Mason? Who's running the shebang?'

'I don't know, and what's more, I don't wanta know. You'll keep your nose out of it if you know what's good for you. It ain't healthy to ask questions. Now get out of here and hightail it back to Dodge.'

Bailey craned forward and looked into the shack to see

Attree moving to the door. He ducked back, and as he moved to the nearest corner to seek concealment a voice called harshly.

'Hey, who in hell are you? What are you doing sneaking around here?'

Bailey moved instantly, lunging for the corner and throwing himself flat as he reached it. He rolled around the corner, thrust up from the ground, and hit a fast run as a gun thundered and muzzle flame burned through the shadows. He pulled his pistol as he ran, and then threw himself down into a depression. The voice was still shouting, and the gun fired again, but Bailey knew his position had not been seen. He stayed low, gun cocked and ready for action, listening to the pandemonium arising in front of the shack.

Mason was yelling for a report of the action. Attree was shouting, and a third voice was calling back an answer.

'I saw a man standing at the back window of the shack. He was looking in at you, Mason. When I challenged him he took off like a greased cat. He's out there somewhere, and I can't see hide or hair of him.'

'Find him,' Mason said. 'I want him.'

Bailey slipped out of his cover and moved away silently in a half-crouch. He headed back to where he had left his horse, listening to the shouting in his rear. He found the animal waiting patiently where he had left it, and breathed a silent prayer of relief as he holstered his gun. He swung into his saddle, and at that moment a dark figure appeared in front of him, seeming to rise up out of the ground.

'Hold it right there,' a harsh voice called. 'I've got you

covered. Get down again, and keep your hands clear of your waist.'

Bailey was tempted to make a try to escape, but a second figure arose some yards to the right of the first man, and he was holding a gun. Bailey heaved a sigh and dismounted. The nearer man struck at him with a pistol. Bailey went down, his senses seeming to explode in pain and shock. He dropped his gun and relaxed into unconsciousness.

FIVE

Bailey was dimly aware of rough hands grasping him and dragging him to his feet. A heavy hand slapped his face and sharp pain cut through his chaotic senses. Two men were talking, their voices making little sense. Bailey heard them in the background but could not understand what they were saying. He sagged in the grip of one man, and a hand kept hitting his face with monotonous regularity.

His senses revived suddenly, and as he emerged from the fog of his shock he reacted instinctively. He kicked the man who was holding him, heard a yell of pain, and then felt the restraining hands falling as the man dropped to the ground. The second man was to Bailey's right. He came lunging forward with his pistol upraised. Bailey ducked to the right and side-stepped the blow. The man's impetus carried him forward and he tripped over his fallen companion. Bailey reached for his pistol and it came to hand with deadly speed.

He bent and struck at the man's head with his gun. There was a satisfactory thud and the man relaxed instantly. Bailey almost lost his balance as he turned to deal with the other, and again his pistol swung. His gun muzzle slammed against the man's head, and suddenly all resistance was gone and he half-crouched, shaking his head and breathing heavily.

Bailey disarmed both men and threw their guns into the surrounding shadows. He went back to his horse and climbed into his saddle. One of the two men got to his feet as Bailey rode away. Bailey touched spurs to his horse and quickly left the area. He saw the lamplight in the shack off to his left and adjusted his direction until he was riding back to Dodge City. His head ached from the blow he had received and he closed his eyes for minutes at a time. It was well after midnight when he saw the lights of Dodge, which guided him into the main street.

Bailey almost fell out of his saddle when he dismounted. He clung to his horse until his senses stopped whirling, and looked about him, wondering why the street around the law office was crowded with people. He caught the unmistakable smell of gun smoke in the air, and spoke to the man nearest him.

'Say, what's going on around here?' he demanded. 'Is it the Fourth of July?'

'The hell it is,' the man replied. 'The law office has been attacked by bad-men, and the prisoners have been released.'

'Where's Buck Stanton?'

'Lying near to death in his office; Doc says he's too bad to be moved.'

Bailey grimaced at the news and tottered forward to the law office. He pushed men aside and made it to the door. A man was standing in the doorway, facing the crowd, keeping them out.

'You can't come in here,' the man said sharply, holding up a hand. He was massively built, with a deep chest, powerful shoulders, and big arms and hands. His Stetson was pushed back off his forehead, revealing fair hair.

'I need to see Buck Stanton. I was doing a job for him.'

'Buck ain't in any condition to worry about his job. The doc is still inside. You better have a word with him.'

Bailey entered the office and paused on the threshold. He saw Stanton lying on his back on the floor, his head resting on a pillow. He was breathing heavily, and the front of his shirt was stained with blood. Three men were standing in the office, talking in low tones. They all looked at Bailey. He recognized the doctor and went forward.

'How's Buck?' he asked. Doc Alwyn shook his head.

'He'll probably make it but it'll be a long job,' Alwyn replied.

'Is he conscious? I need to talk to him.'

Stanton opened his eyes and looked up at Bailey. A weak smile came to his lips. Bailey went close and dropped to one knee. He spoke softly and Stanton closed his eyes.

'Can you hear what I'm saying, Buck?' Bailey demanded.

'Sure. Do you think I'm deaf? Don't take any notice of what Doc says about me. I'll outlive him! So you set eyes on Mason, huh? Why didn't you kill him while you had the chance?'

'I've got no right to do your job.'

'You'd have the right if you let me swear you in. You know as much about what's going on around here as I do, and I'm gonna be on my back for a long spell, so the doc tells me. You've got a personal stake in this business, so grab a law star and pin it on your chest. Arrest everyone who's involved, and keep them in jail until I can get around to handling them. Will you do that? If you wanta get the men who killed your brother then you'll have to get into the fight.'

Bailey considered his experiences of the evening, and nodded. 'Swear me in,' he said firmly, 'and I'll do whatever it takes. Attree will be coming back to town, and he sure deserves to be behind bars. And there are others who have been named.'

'Hold up your right hand.' Stanton stifled a groan as he tried to ease his position on the floor. Bailey held up his right hand and Stanton swore him in. 'It's all yours now,' he said, closing his eyes. 'Do a good job.'

'What happened here?' Bailey asked. 'How did you get shot?'

Stanton opened his eyes. 'A bunch of men came in the office, holding guns. They shot me when I pulled my gun. They unlocked the cells and turned the prisoners loose. Tate is out, and Cates and Kettle. All are in Mason's gang. You'll have to hunt them down.'

Bailey moved to the desk and dropped into the seat behind it. He removed his hat and massaged his head gently. Doc Alwyn came over and examined his head.

'You've taken a hard knock,' he said. 'Come across to my office and I'll look you over.'

'Not right now.' Bailey looked in the drawers of the desk and found a box containing several deputy stars. He pinned one to his chest and got to his feet. 'Is there a night jailer in this town?'

Doc Alwyn nodded. 'That's him by the door. His name is Gus Lantz.'

Bailey went over to the door, where Lantz was keeping the townsmen out of the office.

'You're the night jailer, huh?' Bailey asked.

Lantz looked Bailey up and down, his glasslike blue eyes glinting in the lamplight. He nodded.

'It looks like I'll be the day jailer as well, until Buck is up on his feet again,' he observed. 'You're Bailey, who lost a herd to Nick Mason. I heard about your brother being killed. I'm real sorry about that. If you need a posse to clean up around here then you can call on me any time.'

'Thanks, I'll remember that. Are there any men around who usually form a posse when it's needed?'

'Sure thing! There's Joe Cargill, Frank Nightingale and Rafe Lineker. They are regular posse men. They'll turn out day or night to help the law.'

'I could do with a couple of men to back me right now.' Bailey's eyes glinted as he considered his next move.

'OK. I'll go fetch them. Give me a few minutes, huh?'

'I'll be waiting here.' Bailey nodded and Lantz departed, followed by the two townsmen who had been talking to the doctor. When the door closed behind them the doctor spoke:

'I'd like to put Buck in a cell now. I want to settle him down without too much movement. Will you lend a hand?'

They carried Buck Stanton into the nearest cell and settled him on a bunk. The deputy was asleep now, or unconscious.

'I'll look in on him first thing in the morning,' Alwyn shook his head and took his leave.

Bailey sat down at the desk and looked around, his eyes narrowed as he considered the situation. He reckoned he had done the right thing by pinning on the law star. He needed help to pull in all the suspects on the list in his mind. His patience was running out, and he wanted to settle with the rustlers as soon as possible. He checked his gun and then sat waiting for Lantz to return, his thoughts idling, his brain inundated with grief and the desire for revenge.

The street door was thrust open and Lantz entered the office with two men following. The newcomers were wearing guns, and both were holding shotguns. Lantz introduced them as Cargill and Lineker. Cargill was a tall, thin individual in his forties. His long, thin face was expressionless; his dark eyes half-closed. Lineker was small, fleshy, with a cheerful face and a permanent smile on his lips.

'Lantz told us about the trouble you've had around here,' Lineker said. 'What's the trouble now? Have you found out who turned the prisoners loose?'

Bailey shook his head. 'I've been out on a job for Stanton,' he explained, 'and there are a couple of men in town I want to arrest immediately. I want you two to back me up.'

'That's good.' Cargill nodded. 'It's about time the law stopped pussyfooting around.'

'We're ready for action,' Lineker added. 'Who are the men we're gonna pick up?'

'We'll take them separately. One may not be back in town yet so we'll take him last. We'll go along to the saloon and arrest Ames Hooton.'

'Hooton?' said Lineker with awe in his tone. 'I hope you know what you're doing, Bailey. He's a powerful man around town, and he's got some strong arms backing him.'

'Let's go and get it done.' Bailey got to his feet and led the way to the door.

'Good luck,' said Lantz as they departed.

Only the lamps of Hooton's saloon showed along Main Street as Bailey led the two posse men through the shadows. A chill breeze blew into their faces. Bailey pulled the brim of his Stetson lower on his forehead. He was aching for action, and his right hand was close to the butt of his holstered gun as they moved silently through the dust of the street. When they were level with the door of the saloon, Bailey eased in from the centre of the street to the sidewalk. Someone emerged from the saloon as Bailey stepped up on to the boardwalk, brushing Bailey's shoulder as he departed.

Bailey did not hesitate. He went forward and shouldered the batwings open. The two posse men followed closely as he crossed the threshold of the building. There was just one game of poker in progress at a gaming table, and the five players looked up as the batwings swung. Four men were standing at the bar, talking to the 'tender behind it. There was no sign of Ames Hooton. Bailey guessed the saloon man was in his office, and kept walking across the saloon. When he drew level with the 'tender, he asked:

'Is Hooton in his office?'

'He was when I took him a drink five minutes ago,' the 'tender replied. 'Hey, wait a minute. You can't go in there

71

without an invitation.'

'I've got one.' Bailey drew his pistol and cocked it.

The 'tender remained silent. Bailey reached the door of the office and thrust it open without announcing his presence. He strode inside and Hooton looked up from his desk.

'What's going on?' The saloon man leaned back in his seat.

'I've got an invitation for you,' Bailey replied.

'An invitation?'

'Sure, to visit the law office, so get up and come with us.'

Hooton looked past Bailey; saw Cargill and Lineker standing in the doorway, and his eyes glinted when he read the situation. Cargill was covering the office while Lineker watched the saloon. Both were holding their shotguns ready for action, their attitudes showing that they were ready to start shooting.

'Am I being arrested?' Hooton demanded.

'It sure looks like it,' Cargill said.

'What's the charge?'

'All in good time,' Bailey replied. 'Get up, dump any guns you might have concealed, and come quietly.'

'You can't come in here and drag me off to jail, just like that.' Anger flared in Hooton's eyes and his voice went up a couple of notches.

'If you've a mind to resist then you should be aware that Cargill and Lineker have orders to shoot without hesitation,' Bailey told him.

'Where's Buck Stanton? Why isn't he here?'

'Come with us and all will be explained at the office.

Now get moving.'

Hooton remained in his seat for several fleeting moments while he considered the situation. Then he got to his feet, reached into his left armpit, and produced a small pistol, which he threw on the desk.

'I'm doing this under protest,' he said, 'and someone had better contact Sheldon Lewis, my attorney, pretty damn quick. Tell him to come along to the jail.'

'It will be taken care of,' Bailey agreed.

Hooton left the office with Bailey breathing down his neck. Cargill and Lineker brought up the rear, covering their backs.

'Is everything OK, boss?' demanded the 'tender as they made for the batwings. 'Are you in trouble?'

'What does it look like?' Hooton replied. 'Close up the place, and then tell Lewis to come down to the jail immediately.' He glanced at the poker players sitting near by, who were watching the scene intently. 'Goddam it!' he yelled. 'What do I pay you guys for?' He lunged forward and went down on the floor, shouting as he did so: 'Cut 'em down. Shoot 'em, for Chris'sakes!'

Chairs scraped as the poker players went into action. Bailey lifted his pistol, but paused to see what was happening. When one of the men at the table jerked a gun into view and raised it, Bailey threw down on him and fired, the big .45 recoiling powerfully in his right hand. The man jerked and fell forward across the table.

Cargill cut loose with his shotgun. The fearsome weapon blasted and a whirling load of buckshot caught two of the players. They fell away with blood spurting. The surviving pair of players dropped their guns and raised their hands. Hooton looked up from his position on the floor and then thrust his big body into action. He came up in a rush and made a run for the batwings. Bailey swung his pistol and fired, aiming for the back of the thigh just above the knee. Hooton went back down on the floor and remained there, clutching his leg with both hands; blood spurted between his splayed fingers.

Bailey heard the blast of a shotgun and looked towards the bar in time to see the bar-tender, who had pulled a sawn-off shotgun from under the bar, being hurled backwards by a shot from Lineker's gun. His blood sprayed over the back of the bar as he fell down out of sight.

Gun echoes faded sullenly through the ensuing silence. Bailey stood motionless for an instant, his eyes taking in the shambles of the shooting. Three bodies lay jumbled around the poker table and the other two players were standing motionless with their hands raised. The four men who had been drinking at the bar were also standing motionless with their hands raised. Bailey returned his attention to Hooton. It was time to get the saloon man behind bars.

'Cargill, fetch Doc Alwyn,' he said. 'Lineker, keep an eye on things in here. Shoot anyone who looks like giving trouble.'

Cargill departed swiftly. Bailey stood over Hooton, who looked up at him with pain-filled gaze; blood was seeping from his leg wound.

'Can you walk?' Bailey demanded.

'Can I hell! I'm bleeding to death.'

Bailey went to the bar. One of the four men standing with raised hands looked him in the eye.

'I've got nothing to do with this business,' he said. 'I was just having a quiet drink. Can I leave?'

'Not yet.' Bailey shook his head. 'Stay still and keep quiet.'

A short time later Doc Alwyn hurried into the saloon. He paused on the threshold and looked around in disbelief. Then he approached Hooton, checked that he was not fatally hurt, and went to the gaming table.

'Two are dead, and the other one looks like he won't live through the night,' Alwyn commented. 'What happened?'

'Hooton resisted arrest.' Bailey shrugged. 'Bandage him and then Cargill can put him in a cell. Doc, the 'tender is down behind the bar. Take a look at him. Lineker, do you know a man called Attree?'

'Yeah. Jack Attree. He runs around for Hooton. Do you want him picked up?'

'I followed him out of town earlier, so he may not be back yet.' Bailey reloaded his pistol. 'We'll see to him later. Take a look at the four men at the bar. Do any of them work for Hooton?'

'Not to my knowledge,' Lineker replied.

'And the two survivors of that card game. Where do they fit in around here?'

'They are in Hooton's pay.'

'Then we'll put them behind bars. Cargill, stick around here until we return.' Bailey turned his attention to the two men who had been seated at the table. 'Give me your names,' he said.

'I'm Hank Edgar,' said one, a shifty-eyed, skinny man dressed in a shiny black suit that looked two sizes too large for him. 'I work here in the saloon during the day. I ain't mixed up in any of the goings-on.'

'I'll get around to talking to you later,' Bailey told him. 'Right now you're going to jail.' He looked at the second man. 'Who are you?'

'Jake Turrell. I handle the maintenance job in this place.'

Bailey nodded. 'I'll hold you tonight and talk to you tomorrow. Come on, Lineker; let's take 'em to the jail.'

Bailey told the four men standing at the bar that they were free to go and they departed quickly. The two prisoners were taken to the jail, and Gus Lantz, seated at the desk, looked up when Bailey entered the big office.

'I heard the shooting,' Lantz said. 'What was it all about?'

'Cleaning up.' Bailey shook his head. 'Personally, I've got only one thing on my mind. I want to get the rustlers who killed my brother, and I reckoned it would be a simple case of getting my hands on them. But there are some bad-men around here who are in my way, and I've got to get rid of them before I can settle my own business. A man called Attree was sent out from Dodge earlier to carry a message to Nick Mason. I followed him and found him in cahoots with the rustler. Now I'm cleaning up, and I'm getting mighty impatient because I can't get on with what I want to do.'

'You've got Hank Edgar and Jake Turrell there. They work for Ames Hooton,' Lantz mused. 'That saloon man has a finger in a lot of pies around Dodge. Is he mixed up in this bad business? Or maybe I should ask who isn't?' Lantz reached for the cell keys. 'I'll put them behind bars, no questions asked.'

'Hooton collected a slug in his leg, but he'll be along shortly. I'm going out to pick up a couple more men, and then we'll talk to our prisoners and see what we can come up with.'

Bailey departed with Lineker, and paused on the darkened sidewalk outside the law office.

'I want to pick up Jack Attree. Do you know where he lives?'

'Sure. He's got a shack on the edge of town. He's another who hangs around the saloon.' Lineker's tone was laced with excitement. 'What's he been up to?'

'He led me to Nick Mason when I followed him out of town. I can't wait to talk to him. But he may not be back yet. We'll check his place, and if he hasn't turned up we'll go along to Gruber's place and pick him up.'

'Gruber! Is he in it, too?'

'That's the way it looks right now.' Bailey nodded. 'Let's get it done, huh?'

Lineker made for the edge of town, where complete darkness reigned, but he moved unerringly through the shadows, passing innumerable darkened little buildings in the shanty-town. He halted in front of the last line of shacks and cabins standing on the very edge of Dodge's northern boundary, looked around to get his bearings, and then edged towards a large cabin.

'This is Attree's place,' he said, 'and there's not a light anywhere. I reckon he ain't back yet.'

Bailey tried the thick door. It did not yield to his touch.

'I reckon you're right,' he said. 'So let's go for Gruber.'

As they turned to leave a harsh voice called to them

77

from the shadows surrounding the shack on their left.

'Hold it, you two! What the hell are you doing outside my door? Get your hands up. What's going on?'

'Gruber sent me to fetch you,' Bailey said without hesitation. 'There's been some trouble around here tonight.'

'What kind of trouble?' A figure came forward from the shadows, and Bailey saw a pistol pointing at him.

'Ask Gruber,' Bailey replied. 'I was just told to fetch you.'

'Heck, I've only just got back from seeing Mason, and there was trouble out at his hideout when I was there.'

'Don't complain to me,' Bailey responded. 'Gruber is the boss.'

'Who in hell are you? I ain't seen you around before?'

'We rode out as far as Gruber's ranch earlier,' Bailey informed him, 'and I got that job I was after.'

'Was that you? Heck, Mason thought you were outside his shack earlier. Someone was sneaking around.'

'Not me. I came straight back to town with orders to guard Gruber. I'm only here now because he sent me to get you.'

'OK, so let's go and talk to the man.' Attree thrust his gun into its holster.

As he turned to head for the main street, Bailey palmed his gun and stuck the muzzle into Attree's ribs. 'No,' he said. 'I've got a better idea. Let's go to the law office and talk about what you did tonight.'

Attree halted in his tracks, his right hand dropping to his gun butt.

'You'll never make it,' Bailey told him.

Attree cursed and raised his hands.

'That's smart of you,' Bailey said. 'You know where the law office is so get moving.'

They moved through the shadows to the law office, and Lantz grinned when they entered.

'Hi, Jack,' he greeted Attree. 'It looks like you're in a lot of trouble. I've been waiting for the day I'd see you come in under arrest.'

'Put him in a cell and we'll talk to him later,' Bailey said. 'I've got one more call to make.'

He and Lineker went back along the street. The shadows were dense and the two men moved cautiously. When they reached the land office they entered the alley and ascended the stairs to Gruber's apartment, which was in darkness, and there was no reply to Bailey's knock.

'Looks like he ain't around,' Lineker said.

'We'll pick him up in the morning,' Bailey decided and holstered his gun. 'Let's get back to the office and talk to Attree.'

They descended the stairs, and as Bailey reached the bottom step a red ribbon of muzzle flame slashed through the blackness. The crash of the shot hammered through the intense silence, and Bailey felt a searing pain in his right leg just above the knee. He fell off the step and landed heavily in the alley. A heavy object thudded against his head and he lost consciousness with the reverberations of the shot hammering against his ears.

SIX

Bailey experienced a period of pain and confusion when he opened his eyes. He was in darkness and lying on his back on hard ground. Above him stars shone remotely, seeming to undulate as he gazed at them. His head ached intolerably. His right leg was filled with agony, and it was some time before he recovered sufficiently to recall the shooting. He rolled on to his right side and braced his left leg. His right leg did not seem to want to move and he was tempted to take the line of least resistance and lie still. But he needed to get back to the law office.

At that moment he remembered Lineker, and called the man's name. There was no reply. The night breeze blew into his face. He fought against inertia. Thoughts of his dead brother entered his mind, jerked him from his shock, and he began to move. He discovered that he could not put weight on his right leg, and as he tried to get to his feet a cautious voice called from the shadows.

'Who's that over there? Speak up. I've got you covered.'

'I'm Bailey, the new deputy. I've been shot. Get Lantz from the law office.'

'This is Lantz.'

'Where's Lineker?'

'I ain't seen him since you two left the office. I heard the shooting, and when you didn't show up I reckoned there was something wrong. Hold on a minute. I'll get a light.'

Bailey heard receding footsteps, and sat on the ground holding his right thigh with both hands. He could feel blood seeping from his wound and used his neckerchief to stanch the flow. Moments later Lantz returned carrying a lantern, and when Bailey looked around he saw Lineker lying motionless several yards away. Lantz cursed and hurried to Lineker's side, bent over him, and then straightened.

'Linker's dead,' he said harshly.

Bailey turned cold. He clenched his teeth, aware that the pain in his breast was sharper than the discomfort of his wound. He looked around and saw that he was in the alley, beside Gruber's stairs, and wondered who had ambushed him and where Gruber was at that moment.

'I'd better get you to the doc's place,' Lantz said. 'Where are you hit?'

'I caught it in the right thigh. I think I've stopped the bleeding. Help me up and let's get moving.'

Lantz pulled Bailey to his feet and thrust a shoulder into his left armpit. Bailey found that by using Lantz as a prop he could limp along with a little difficulty and a lot of pain. They left the alley and headed for the doctor's house, which was in darkness. Bailey leaned against a wall while Lantz roused the doctor, and eventually Alwyn opened the front door.

Bailey endured the doctor's ministrations, and Alwyn

finally bandaged the wound.

'You'll have to keep off the leg for a few days,' he said. 'Rest up as much as you can. I'll change the dressing tomorrow.'

'I'll be at the law office,' Bailey told him. 'Where's Stanton, and how is he?'

'He's sleeping in one of the cells in the jail. I'll see how he is tomorrow before I think about moving him.'

'And where is Hooton?'

'He's locked in a cell. You don't have to worry about him.'

Bailey nodded. Lantz helped him across the street, and Cargill opened the street door of the office to them. Cargill cursed when he heard about Lineker.

'I'll go and see to him,' he said. 'Have you got any idea who shot you?'

'I didn't see anyone.' Bailey sat down at the desk, and sighed heavily as he stuck out his right leg to ease the pain. 'We went to pick up Gruber. He wasn't in his apartment, and the shooting came out of the shadows as we left.'

'If I see Gruber shall I arrest him?' Cargill asked.

'No. He'll keep. I'll get to him when I can. And I've got to get back to my own business. I've got half a herd on Gruber's range, and another half was heading back to Dodge the last time I saw their tracks. I need to find them, but quick.'

'You heard what Doc said,' Lantz reminded him. 'Keep off that leg for a few days.'

'Help me into the cells and I'll rest,' Bailey replied. 'I wanta be out on the range at first light, looking for my stock.'

Lantz shrugged. He assisted Bailey into the cell block and eased him down on a bunk. Bailey closed his eyes, and despite the pain throbbing through his thigh, he drowsed into sleep until dawn.

When he opened his eyes he heaved a sigh of relief because the night was over. But frustration filled him when he levered himself up off the bunk to discover that his leg was too painful to support him. He sat down heavily and endured a shaft of pure agony that stabbed through the limb.

Lantz came through from the office.

'How you doing?' he demanded.

'Not so good. I can't put any weight on the leg this morning. How in hell am I gonna move around?'

'The easiest way is to do what Doc ordered – rest up until it's better. But I can see you won't do that, so I'll go along to the carpenter shop and ask Charlie Fenton to make you a crutch. It won't take him more than a couple of minutes, and it'll be better than nothing.'

'Help me into the front office,' Bailey said.

He felt easier sitting at the desk with a chair pulled forward to rest his right foot. Lantz departed, and as he opened the door a woman's voice bade him good morning and Stella Pearson entered the office. She confronted Bailey, her face showing grave concern.

'It's all over town that you were shot last night,' she said, staring at the bandage on his thigh. His pants leg had been slit open and was now pinned together. 'Is it bad?'

'I can endure it,' he replied. 'But right now I can't put any weight on it, and I need to be out on the range looking for the rest of my stock. I can't afford to waste any more time. Those rustlers are moving fast.'

Stella shook her head. 'It's my fault this has happened,' she said. 'If you hadn't got involved in my problems you would have handled your own trouble by now.'

Bailey shook his head. 'Your problems are not to blame,' he told her. 'I got mixed up with the law; that was my problem, and by the time I'll be able to walk again my cows will be long gone.'

'You helped me, so the least I can do is help you. I'll ride out and track your herd.'

Bailey shook his head emphatically. 'No! That ain't a job for a woman. I won't let you do it.'

She smiled. 'I didn't ask you if I could; I told you I would. And how could you stop me, stuck in that chair?'

'This is a serious business,' he said. 'If you came up against the rustlers they wouldn't care that you're a woman. They'd shoot you like they shot my brother.'

She saw the grief that shone in his eyes and that made her more determined. 'I can ride where I like on the range,' she said, 'and no one would suspect that I was looking for rustled stock. If I find anything out there I'll come back and let you know.'

'Please don't do that,' he said. 'I can handle the chore when I'm back on my feet.'

'I have to go out to our ranch today, so I'll take a look around. See you later.'

She turned on her heel and departed. Bailey pushed himself to his feet as the street door closed, and then fell back into his seat, cursing the pain flaring in his leg. Of all the rotten luck, he thought. He had things to do and could not even walk.

84

Lantz returned within an hour, smiling, carrying a wooden crutch.

'This will get you moving,' he said. 'We're about the same height so Charlie measured me. He said you'd need something on the top to pad your armpit, and said to tell you not try to run with it.'

'I'll be lucky if I can walk with it,' Bailey observed sourly.

He got to his feet and stood with his right foot raised while he put the crutch under his right armpit. When he eased his weight on the crutch he was able to stand easily, and his wound did not complain. He stomped around the office to get accustomed to the crutch, and then headed for the door. He paused to check his pistol, and his expression showed determination when he opened the door.

'I need some breakfast,' he said. 'Then I'm gonna ride my horse. If I can sit my saddle then I'll be moving out after the rustlers. I've got to locate my herd.'

'What about the situation here?' Lantz demanded. 'I'm only the jailer. I don't know the first thing about questioning prisoners.'

'They'll keep until I get back,' Bailey told him.

'And what should be done about Gruber?'

'I'll look him up before I ride out.'

'Hooton wants to see his lawyer. What do I do if the lawyer says Hooton has to be released?'

'Stick the lawyer in a cell until I get back,' Bailey retorted.

He negotiated the sidewalk fairly well, and paused outside the land office, which was unlocked. He entered the office and paused at the bottom of the stairs leading to Gruber's apartment. There was no sign of life. He saw a

85

bloodstain in the dust where he had fallen the night before, then turned and went on his way. He stopped at the diner for breakfast, and then went on to the livery barn. Pete McKay emerged from his office.

'I heard you had died,' McKay said.

'You heard wrong. As far as I know I'm still breathing. Can you tell me if Gruber, the land agent, left town last evening?'

'He sure did, and in one hell of a hurry.'

'Did he say where he was going, or when he would be back?'

'Not a word. He burned up the trail heading north, so I reckoned he was making for his ranch.'

'Did he ride alone?'

'He did.'

Bailey considered for a moment. 'Saddle my horse for me,' he said at length. 'I can't manage that, and I need to be riding.'

McKay readied Bailey's horse for travel. When he tightened the cinch he shook his head. 'You sure won't be able to swing that leg over the horse,' he observed. 'You better come out back and climb the corral. That way you should make it. But if you have to get off the horse you sure as hell won't get back on it again in a hurry.'

'I'll worry about that if it happens.' Bailey followed McKay out back and eased up on to the top rail of the corral. McKay brought the horse alongside, and Bailey managed to scramble into the saddle without creating too much pain.

'What you gonna do about the crutch?'

'I'll pick it up when I get back. Has Stella Pearson

ridden out this morning?'

'Yeah, she was another who was in a tearing hurry to shake the dust of the town off her boots. I don't know what's going on around here.' Mackay shook his head as he carried the crutch through to his office.

Bailey set off, and experienced several pain-filled minutes before he settled his right leg into a more comfortable position and transferred most of his weight to his left side. He travelled at a lope and left town. When he reached the trail north he pushed the horse faster, and his impatience faded when he hit a good pace.

He made for the spot where his cows had been split into two smaller herds, and, reaching it, he paused to consider his next move. Stella had said she was going to her ranch, and he headed in that direction, determined to dissuade her from checking on his stock. He caught sight of her as she was riding into the ranch yard, and a frown came to his face when she rode into the barn behind the house, for as she entered the building he caught a movement out of the corner of his eye and saw two riders moving in from the far side of the yard. He pulled to one side, gained cover, and kept moving. The two men were approaching covertly, and he noted that one of them was holding a rifle at the ready across his saddle.

Bailey drew his pistol and sent his horse along the right-hand side of the house. He reined in at the rear corner and looked across the back yard to the door of the barn, which was standing open. The two riders had reached the door, and one halted his horse in the doorway while the other rode into the barn.

Bailey cursed his luck because he could not dismount.

He started across the back yard, his horse moving at a walk, his pistol held ready, covering the rider in the doorway, and as he drew nearer he was startled by a gunshot that hammered inside the barn. He shook his reins instantly and sent his horse lunging forward. The rider in the doorway turned at the sound of hoofs on the hardpan of the yard and began to swing his horse to face Bailey because his rifle was across his saddle and pointing in the wrong direction.

'Drop it!' Bailey yelled.

The rider ignored his call, and Bailey squeezed the trigger as the blade of his foresight lined up on the figure. The bullet thudded into the man's chest and he uttered a cry and slipped sideways out of his saddle. Bailey guided his mount into the barn. Blue gun smoke was drifting across the interior, and he squinted to get a look at the situation inside. He reined in quickly. The second rider was down on his back, and Stella was crouching in cover, a big Colt .44 pistol gripped in her right hand, its muzzle covering Bailey.

'Don't shoot,' Bailey called.

Stella lowered the pistol and came forward, her expression showing disbelief.

'What are you doing here?' she demanded. 'That was a fool thing to do, riding in here like that. I thought you were one of his friends.'

'There is another. I had to shoot him. What happened here?'

'He rode in on me, and wasn't expecting me to have a gun. It looked like he was gonna shoot me for no reason at all. What's going on?'

Bailey rode forward to peer down at the lifeless man. 'Heck, this is one of the men who got busted out of jail last night. I arrested him. His name is Tate. He's one of the rustlers. Let's take a look at the one I shot.'

He rode out of the barn. looked at the dead man in the dust and recognized him. 'This is another escaped prisoner,' he mused. 'So what is he doing here?'

'They were waiting for me,' Stella said. 'Gruber wants us out of the ranch and it looks like they are doing his dirty work.'

'I tried to pick up Gruber last night but he wasn't in town. He left in a hurry, as if he expected trouble. There's something going on there that ain't easy to piece together. I'd better take a look around in case there are more hardcases in the area. Get what you came for and I'll see you safely on your way back to town before I look for my herd. And when you get back to town stay there. You can see it ain't safe for you out here until this trouble is over.'

'I need to get some clothes,' she said tonelessly, and Bailey could see that she was scared. 'I'll stay in town after this, and stay out of trouble.'

Bailey nodded and touched spurs to his horse. He rode out, circled the ranch looking for hoof tracks, and soon located them. He tracked the two dead men's prints to a deserted camp on a ridge overlooking the ranch, and as he rode into the camp a horse started running out of a nearby stand of timber, its rider hunched over in the saddle. Bailey cursed and set off in pursuit.

His quarry pulled away until fifty yards separated them, and Bailey soon realized that he could not gain on the man. His wound was hurting intolerably, and he had to

89

slow down and content himself with following tracks.

It didn't take him long to see that the rider was heading in the general direction of Gruber's ranch. He thought of Stella, waiting at her ranch to head back to town, and closed his mind to that particular situation, hoping she would be wise enough to leave as soon as she could. He was still being side-tracked from his personal problems, but the opportunity of catching Gruber flat-footed and making an arrest appealed to him so he kept riding.

He was too far away from his quarry to get a good look at him, and did not want to ride into the ranch and then find himself knee-deep in Gruber's men. When the ranch came into view he swung away to the right and rode for cover. He watched his quarry ride into the yard and head for the house. Moments later Gruber emerged from the house and stood on the porch, listening intently to the man's report.

Bailey glanced around, wanting to get closer to the ranch house, and saw that he would have to dismount if he wanted to do so. He discounted the knowledge. His crutch was back in Dodge, and he could not get back on the horse once he got down. He rode into a draw that angled towards the ranch house and came to a halt within fifty feet of the back yard. He looked around and finally spotted a tree stump that might enable him to dismount. He scrambled out of the saddle and hung on to the saddle horn as he slid down until his feet touched the ground.

He took his rifle along as he inched over rough ground with most of his weight on his left leg. Only the toe of his right boot touched earth. But the pain increased in his leg and he was soon forced to halt. He dropped flat and used brute strength to drag his aching body up the side of the draw. The ranch house was now merely twenty yards away, and the sight of it mocked him as he looked around help-lessly.

Riders began leaving the ranch, and when they spread out into an ever widening circle he knew they were intent on locating him. He waited until they were clear of the ranch before dragging his body erect. Sweat broke out on his forehead when he tried to walk, and he clung to a con-venient branch to keep on his feet. He began to have second thoughts about the wisdom of his decision to take Gruber into custody, and considered how much valuable time he was wasting, realizing that he was trying to do something he was physically unfit for when he should have been concentrating on his rustled stock.

Frustration boiled through him as he turned and went back to his horse. He slithered down into the draw and untied his mount. When he positioned the animal beside the stump it wouldn't stand still as he tried to gain the saddle. After several vain attempts to mount he clung to the saddle horn, gasping for breath.

A harsh laugh sounded and he looked around quickly, reaching for his gun.

'Hold it, unless you're itching to die,' a voice com-manded.

He saw two riders sitting their horses on the opposite rim of the draw. Both were pointing guns at him. One was laughing, and waggled his gun. He was large and fleshy, dressed in range clothes, and had a yellow neckerchief tied at his throat. The other was a smaller man with a steady gun and a killer's cold gaze.

'You sure tried hard to get into that saddle, mister, and it looked real funny from here. If you'd have asked us, we'd have helped you into leather. We've been looking for you. So get rid of your guns and Donovan will come down and hump you into the saddle.'

Bailey dropped his pistol, pulled his Winchester out of the saddle scabbard and leaned it against the stump. Donovan dismounted and came slithering down into the draw. He held his hands together and Bailey put his left foot into the hands and was thrust up until he could swing his right leg over the saddle. Agony filled the limb as his weight hit leather. He gripped the saddle horn until the pain subsided.

Donovan took hold of Bailey's reins and led the horse up the draw to a game trail in the right-hand wall, which led them up to the range. The other man was waiting with the horses, and Bailey was compelled to ride with them to the ranch. As they rode across to the porch Gruber came out of the house and stood waiting to receive him.

'Where did you find him, Waco?' Gruber demanded before they reached him. His face showed extensive bruising from Bailey's earlier attack in Dodge City.

'He was skulking in the draw, and had a rifle with him,' Waco replied. 'It looked like he was trying to get into a position to take a shot at you, boss.'

'Get him down off that horse and make sure he's got no other weapons on him. Then hogtie him. After I've talked to him you can take him out to a quiet place, kill him, and bury him where he won't be found. Be careful. He's smart enough to get the better of you.'

Bailey groaned in agony when he was dragged from the

saddle. Rough hands searched him. Then his hands were tied behind his back. Gruber motioned to a chair on the porch and the two men thrust him into it. Gruber drove his fist into Bailey's face, and then stepped back and kicked his outstretched injured leg. Bailey gritted his teeth to prevent an outcry.

'I owe you that,' Gruber said. 'I knew my time would come if I waited long enough.'

'You've never said a truer word,' Bailey grated. He could feel blood leaking from his left eyebrow. 'Your days are numbered, Gruber, but you don't know it. If you go back to Dodge you'll be arrested on sight.'

'What the hell are you talking about? I haven't broken the law.'

'How do you explain my rustled stock?'

'I had nothing to do with that.'

'They were found on your range, herded by two of your men. It's an open and shut case.'

'If what you say is true then I've been set up.'

'Prove it. You don't act like an honest man. You've been getting at the smaller ranchers, trying to force them to sell out. I saw what happened at the Pearson ranch. Your gunhand shot Mike Pearson without warning, and would have killed him if Stella Pearson hadn't shot him dead. You've got a lot of awkward questions to answer, Gruber.'

'You won't be around to hear my answers.' Gruber looked at his two men. 'Get him out of here, well away from the ranch, and bury him deep.'

'Now see here, Gruber,' Waco said instantly. 'We draw gun wages for fighting your enemies. We don't get paid for cold-blooded murder.'

93

Bailey looked at the gunman, filled with sudden hope.

'So what's your price?' Gruber demanded.

'A hundred bucks; cash in hand.'

'Wait here and I'll get the dough.' Gruber went into the house.

'Come on, Donovan.' Waco motioned to his pard. 'Let's get him back in his saddle.'

They manhandled Bailey off the porch and thrust him into his saddle. Gruber emerged from the house clutching a sheaf of notes, and pushed them into Waco's ready hand. 'Get it done,' Gruber said, and went back into the house.

Bailey slumped in his saddle as he was led out of the yard. It looked bad for him, and he could see no way out of his predicament. . . .

SEVEN

As they left the ranch Bailey groaned with each step his horse took. They headed out across the range, riding at a lope. Waco rode beside him and Donovan followed behind. A rider appeared on their left and fired a shot into the air. Bailey tensed and his hopes rose. Waco dragged Bailey's horse to a halt and they waited for the rider to arrive. Bailey's hopes dropped to zero when the newcomer, a dark-faced hardcase, reined in, grinning.

'So you got him, Waco,' he declared. 'Where are you taking him?'

'Howdy, Fenner. This is his last ride. Gruber wants him buried.'

'I'll call off the search and bring in the rest of the crew.' Fenner turned his horse and rode off.

Bailey watched him go. It seemed that cold-blooded murder was acceptable to Gruber's crew. He glanced at Waco's hard expression. The man caught his glance and grinned.

'It won't be long now, Bailey. Your worries will soon be over.'

'You're getting a hundred bucks to kill me,' Bailey responded. 'I'll pay a lot more than that to stay alive.'

'Nice try! But I've got Gruber's money in my pocket and I'll do the job I've been paid for. How much do you think your life is worth?'

'It's worth a lot more than one hundred bucks.'

'Put a figure on it.'

'Five hundred bucks. That's all I've got until I get the dough for my herd.'

'You ain't got a herd no more, and we've already been paid for stealing it.'

'You're admitting to rustling my herd?'

Waco nodded. 'Sure, why not? You can't do anything about it. In half an hour you'll be dead and buried.'

'So who killed my brother and my pard?'

'Hell, I don't know! I was up front with the lead steers when we ran the herd out. I heard shots but didn't see what happened. We had our work cut out because we took the steers in the storm.'

Bailey grimaced, recalling the storm and his brother dying. He tested the ropes binding his wrists behind his back, but there was no slack in them. He glanced around and despair filtered through him. For the first time in his life he felt completely helpless. If he hadn't been tied he would have taken any chance to survive. He slumped in the saddle, ignoring the pain throbbing in his right leg. His only hope was that he would be untied before they shot him, for he would tackle them, no matter how slim his chances.

'How much further are we going?' Donovan called.

'To the river,' Waco replied. 'I know where there's a

quicksand. It swallowed a steer last fall without leaving a sign of it. I thought we'd throw him in there, else we'll have to go to the trouble of digging a hole for him, and I ain't about to do that. It ain't far now so shut up and keep coming, unless you wanta go back now and leave me to finish the job alone.'

'And you'll get to keep all the dough Gruber gave you!' Donovan guffawed. 'You're a sly one, Waco, but I'll stick. Gruber gave that dough to get the job done, and I've got half of it coming my way.'

Bailey shivered at the prospect. He had once seen a steer sucked down in a quicksand, and recalling the incident sent a pang of fear through him. Waco quickened his pace then, and they went on at a faster rate. Bailey clenched his teeth as every nerve in his body protested at the way he was going to die.

When the river was sighted, Waco yelled and waved an arm.

'There it is,' he crowed. 'All I've got to do is find the spot.' He grinned at Bailey. 'It won't be long now.'

'We don't have to go to all that bother,' Donovan said. 'Why don't we just throw him in and shoot him full of holes? The river will carry him for miles, and he'll wind up where no one will know who the hell he is.'

'I fancy watching him in the quicksand, slowly sinking down as he's sucked in.' Waco grinned. 'I've seen cattle die like that, but never a man. It'll make good watching.'

They reined in on the riverbank. Trees lined the waterway. The river was fast-flowing, and sunlight glittered on the surface. Waco looked around, shaking his head.

'I think the spot I'm looking for is downstream from

here,' he mused. 'I'll ride that way and take a look. Hold him here, Donovan. No need for all of us to ride. I'll fire three shots if I find it, and if I don't I'll come back and we'll ride upstream.'

Bailey became alert when Waco rode off. He glanced at Donovan, who relaxed, took a sack of Bull Durham from a pocket in his shirt, and began to roll the makings sighing contentedly when smoke spiralled around his head. He grinned at Bailey.

'It ain't worth wasting a smoke on you,' he said, 'seeing that you'll be dead in a few minutes.'

Bailey tried again to loosen the rope around his wrists, but to no avail. He slumped in his saddle. It looked as if his time had run out, and regret filled him as the moments passed. Right now, he would settle for being able to kill the man who had shot Thad. He thought of his brother, dead before his time, and the killer free and still breathing God's good air. He looked at Donovan.

'Were you on the rustling raid the other evening?' he demanded.

'Sure I was.' Donovan flicked his cigarette stub into the swirling water.

'Two drovers were killed. Did you shoot them?'

'No. I was with the men that ran off the cattle. It was a rough night – all the wind and rain, and when shots were fired at us Frank Hayman cut loose until there was no more shooting from the drovers. Yeah, I reckon Hayman killed them. He always took care of the herders. He said it gave him a kick when they fell out of their saddles.'

'One of them was my brother,' Bailey raged. 'Who is Hayman? He's the man who runs the land agent's office with Gruber in Dodge, ain't he?'

'That's him, sure enough. Gruber sends him along with us just to count the cattle we steal. I reckon they don't trust us.'

'I saw him out at the Pearson ranch with Gruber when Mike Pearson was shot by Gruber's gun man,' Bailey mused. 'Hell, Hayman doesn't look the kind of man to kill in cold blood.'

'He's the kind that can't bear watching someone being killed, but he's different when he's doing the killing.' Donovan shrugged. 'He's been on many raids with us, and always does the shooting. Anyway, what does it matter? You ain't gonna get to him. You'll be gone very shortly. I can see Waco coming back so I guess the spot he's looking for is upstream.'

Bailey looked over his shoulder and saw the gunman returning. His spirits sank to zero. The thought of being shot down like a helpless rat, with his hands tied behind his back, was hard to accept. This was a living nightmare which he found impossible to accept. His heart began to pound, and he looked around wildly for some means of escape. His mind seemed to burn with Hayman's name. He couldn't face the thought of dying without avenging Thad's death.

'It ain't downstream,' Waco remarked, reining in beside Bailey. 'We'll have to go the other way.'

'Why in hell bother?' Donovan demanded. 'This is as good a spot as any. I say let's throw him in the river, shoot him full of holes, and have done with it. I've had enough of this.'

'And spoil my fun?' Waco shook his head.

Bailey listened to them wrangling about how and where he should die.

'Come on, let's get it done.' Waco led the way upstream.

They had to skirt trees and vegetation growing on the bank of the river and flourishing right down to the water's edge. Waco rode around a large thicket ahead of Bailey, and Bailey was beside Donovan, and between him and the thicket.

A movement on Bailey's left attracted his attention. He glanced sideways and saw a rider hunched over in his saddle in the thicket, and he was holding a pistol. Bailey stiffened as he recognized the newcomer. It was Joe Cargill, the posse man from Dodge City. Cargill grinned as their glances locked, and as Bailey rode by his position he touched spurs to the flanks of his mount and came out of the thicket behind them. He levelled his gun at the unsuspecting Donovan, but held his fire.

'Shoot him, Cargill,' Bailey rapped. 'They're gonna kill me.'

Donovan twisted in his saddle, reached for his gun and drew it with unbelievable speed. Bailey held his breath, expecting each moment to be his last. Then Cargill's pistol blasted. The crash of the shot had Waco, ten yards ahead, turning in his saddle as Cargill's slug smacked into Donovan. Blood spurted. Donovan went over backwards and fell heavily. One foot caught in a stirrup and he was dragged away by his startled horse.

Bailey's horse cavorted, almost throwing him from the saddle. He gripped the animal with his knees and retained his seat as it took out after Donovan's horse. Cargill started after Bailey, who shouted over his shoulder.

'Kill the other one! Nail him, Cargill.'

At that moment Waco opened fire at Cargill, who jumped from his saddle and stepped behind his horse for cover. He aimed his pistol across the saddle and fired two shots. His first bullet whipped Waco's Stetson from his head. The second struck Waco's gun hand and he lost his grip on the weapon. Waco reached into a pocket and produced a smaller calibre, short barrelled pistol. He spurred his horse, and came galloping at Cargill, shooting fast and yelling.

Cargill aimed for Waco's horse and fired. The animal was hit in the head and went down quickly, turning a somersault before sliding and rolling to a stop. Waco kicked his feet out of his stirrups to jump clear, but his left foot caught and he was under the horse when it hit the ground. He was motionless, his neck broken, and echoes of the shots faded away into the distance.

Bailey managed to calm his horse. The animal had stopped close to the spot where Donovan was lying. Donovan's horse had halted and was grazing near by. Bailey almost fell to the ground as reaction set in. He gripped the horse with his knees and watched Cargill coming towards him. He took a quick look around at his surroundings, mindful of the fact that Gruber had sent out his crew to look for him.

'They were gonna kill you?' Cargill demanded as he came up.

'I thought my last moment had come. Cut me loose and give me a gun. There are men out from Gruber's ranch looking for me. How did you happen to be out here, and right on the spot to save me?'

101

'You've got Lantz to thank for that. He told me to keep an eye on you. I trailed you to the Pearson ranch, and got there just after the shooting. Stella told me what happened, and said you'd gone out to check for more trouble. I trailed along behind you, and saw what happened at Gruber's place. When these two hardcases brought you out here I trailed along to take a hand when it looked like you were about to get yourself killed.'

Cargill cut the rope binding Bradley, and fetched Donovan's pistol and rifle. Bailey gripped the weapons, overwhelmed by relief. He checked the pistol, discovered it was fully loaded, and slid it into his empty holster. The Winchester had only two cartridges in the magazine, and he opened his saddlebag and loaded the long gun.

'What will we do with these bodies?' Cargill asked. 'Do we take them back to town?'

'I'm not going back to town. I've got some steers to locate. Some are on Gruber's range, but half the herd was driven off in another direction, and I intend to find them.'

'And Gruber?'

'He'll keep till later. He won't run. He's got too much to lose. Maybe you should go back to Dodge and tell Lantz what happened out here.'

Cargill shook his head. 'I got my orders and I'll stick to them,' he said. 'We'll ride together.'

Bailey nodded. 'We've got to get away from here. You know this range better than I do. Can we get back to the Pearson ranch without showing ourselves?'

'If we ride to the left and follow the river until we reach Henry Wescott's ranch, we'll have a straight run back to the Pearson place. How's the leg holding out?'

'I should have followed the doctor's orders and stayed off it, but I can't afford the time. I've got this far so I'll keep on.' Bailey turned his horse and they followed the course of the river.

A couple of hours later Cargill reined in and looked around. Bailey removed his Stetson, wiped his forehead, and dried the inside of the hat before replacing it on his head.

'We're clear of Gruber's range,' Cargill said. 'But we'll have to watch out for Westcott's crew. They don't like strangers wandering over their grass.'

'This Westcott, is he the one who runs the cattle-buying business in Dodge?'

'The same. His brother Tim's got a meat-packing business in Dodge. They got a lot of other business interests as well.'

'I had a deal with Henry Westcott for my herd before it got stolen.' Bailey studied his surroundings with a cold gaze, his mind filled with an urge to look up Frank Hayman.

'Let's keep moving,' Cargill suggested.

They went on, Cargill pointing out the way. They crossed the range, and came eventually to the Pearson ranch, which was deserted. Bailey took over then, heading along the trail to find the spot where his herd had been split. He found it eventually, and Cargill dismounted to check prints. When he returned to where Bailey was sitting his horse he shook his head.

'Those steers are heading for Dodge,' he said. 'What do you make of it?'

'Let's follow the tracks and find out.' Bailey touched

103

spurs to his horse.

They followed until they saw Dodge City in the distance.

'I don't understand this,' Bailey mused. 'Half the stock remained close to Gruber's ranch house and the rest have been driven in this direction.'

'The answer will be at the end of these tracks,' Cargill opined. 'But it looks pretty plain to me. The rustlers split up the herd; half went to Gruber as his share, and the rest are on their way to Tim Wescott's slaughterhouse. It looks like they're gonna be sold there.'

'I reckon Nick Mason is out to get his share,' Bailey mused. 'He's pushed the steers in to sell them. It looks like a pretty big steal has been going on around here. Gruber's involved and so is Henry Westcott and his brother. And where does Nick Mason fit into this?'

'I wouldn't know, but it looks like you've got it figured right.' Cargill nodded. 'You said you saw Mason in Gruber's line shack, so he's certainly in with Gruber. We'd better go on and see what's at the end of these tracks.'

They followed the trail to the cattle pens at the back of a large barnlike building on the outskirts of Dodge.

'This is Tim Westcott's slaughterhouse, and next to it is his meat-packing business. It looks like your steers have gone inside.' Cargill's tone was harsh. He looked around intently. 'There ain't anything to prove the cattle have ever been here.'

'Except their track.' Bailey made an effort to dismount but changed his mind instantly. The pain in his leg was intolerable. He looked around helplessly.

'What do you wanta do?' Cargill asked, watching him closely.

'I want to go inside and talk to the boss man. He'll have all the answers.'

'I can handle that.' Cargill slid out of his saddle.

'Hold it. If they've got my cattle in here as rustled stock then the moment you talk to them about it they are gonna start shooting, so I'm the one who'll handle the chore.'

'You can't put your weight on your leg,' Cargill observed.

'I left a crutch with the livery man this morning when I rode out. You could fetch it from him, and we'll face these galoots together.'

'Sounds like a good idea.' Cargill grinned and remounted. 'Give me five minutes.'

He rode off and Bailey tried to ease his weight in the saddle. His right leg was badly cramped and the pain of it was becoming intolerable. He positioned his horse close to the corral fence and transferred his weight out of the saddle. He got both feet out of the stirrups, and placed his left foot on a convenient pole of the corral. When he shifted his weight to his left leg he discovered that he could not move his right leg. He hung on to the corral pole and urged the horse to move forward. It took a tentative step and then slid out from under him.

Bailey sat on the top rail of the corral and waited impatiently for Cargill to return. The sound of a heavy door slamming attracted his attention and he looked at the building and saw two men emerging from inside. They were wearing long white coats, and one of them had a large bloodstain down the front of his. The other was carrying a rifle with the butt in his right armpit, the muzzle pointing at the ground. Bailey stiffened as they came

105

towards him, and eased his right hand to the butt of his holstered pistol.

'Why are you hanging around here?' demanded the man with the rifle. He was big and flashy, his manner suggesting that he was accustomed to giving orders.

'He's wearing a deputy sheriff badge, Tully,' observed the other man, who was undersized and skinny. 'It looks like he trailed those cows in here.'

'Were they steers wearing the Double B brand?' Bailey asked.

Tully began lifting the muzzle of the long gun to cover him, and Bailey set his right hand into motion. He palmed his gun, and squeezed off a shot as his foresight lined up on Tully, who was suddenly desperate to complete his movement. Bailey's gun jerked and a puff of smoke accompanied the blasting crash of the shot. A splotch of blood appeared on Tully's white coat in the centre of the chest. His rifle exploded, but the muzzle was still depressed and the 44.40 slug kicked up dirt at the bottom of the corral. Tully dropped the rifle, twisted sharply, and fell on his face.

Bailey shifted his aim to cover the second man, who raised his hands instantly. His manner changed as he looked into the muzzle of the pistol, and he cringed, his face expressing desperation.

'Don't shoot!' he gasped. 'I'm only the slaughterman here. I do my job and nothing more. I ain't broken the law.'

'What's your name?' Bailey demanded.

'I'm Frank Duthie.'

'So tell me about the cattle that came in earlier. How

were they branded?'

'It was like you said, a double B.'

'Who brought them in?'

'I don't know who they were. Three riders showed up and put the stock in the corral. I happened to look out of the office window when they arrived. One of them came in to report their arrival and I signed a receipt for them. That's all I can tell you. Were they rustled stock?'

'You better believe it! Describe the man who came into your office.'

Duthie stammered through a description which brought an image of Nick Mason, the rustler boss, to Bailey's mind.

'We'll wait here a few moments before going in to see your boss. He's Tim Westcott, huh?'

'Sure, but you're barking up the wrong tree if you think he'd do anything against the law.'

The thud of hoofs attracted Bailey's attention and he looked over his shoulder to see Cargill emerging from an alley. He was carrying Bailey's crutch, and grinned as he reined in beside them.

'You've been busy,' he observed.

Bailey slid down from the corral and took the crutch, leaning the weight of his right side on it and raising his right foot from the ground. A handhold had been fastened to the crutch and he gripped it and swung his right leg slowly to ease the pain in the limb.

'Let's get moving,' he said at length. 'Lead the way, Duthie. Take me to Westcott.'

'He ain't gonna like this,' Duthie said.

'Let me worry about that,' Bailey told him.

They entered the building and traversed a passage that led to a set of offices. Duthie knocked at a door and a voice bade him enter.

'You'd better wait out here and prevent anyone busting in on me,' Bailey suggested, and Cargill nodded.

Bailey pushed Duthie ahead and entered a big room which had a large window overlooking Main Street. There was a desk by the window, and a big, fleshy man was seated behind it. At first Bailey thought he was facing Henry Westcott, the man who had contracted to buy his herd before it was stolen, but this brother was younger, and his hair was a different colour.

Tim Westcott maintained an expressionless face. He was in his forties, dressed for the part he occupied in the local community – a successful businessman. His blue store suit was immaculate. He wore a red cravat with a glinting diamond stick pin showing prominently. Bailey noted a bulge in his left armpit, where a pocket gun nestled.

'What's your business?' demanded Westcott curtly, his gaze on the deputy sheriff badge pinned to Bailey's shirt-front.

'I'm tracking steers that were stolen a couple of nights ago,' Bailey replied.

'And you think they came in here?' Westcott leaned forward, rested his elbows on the desk, and cupped his chin in his hands.

'I know they did. Their tracks came right up to your back door.'

'What's this all about, Duthie?' Westcott turned his gaze to the slaughterman.

'He mentioned a herd branded with Double B, boss.'

'And did those cows come in here?'

'Yes. McCluskey delivered two hundred head earlier this afternoon, and they were wearing the Double B brand.'

'Did you give McCluskey a receipt for them?' Westcott did not seem unduly troubled by the situation.

'Sure I did, boss. It's normal procedure. We wouldn't have a leg to stand on if I didn't get a signed receipt.'

Westcott nodded, lifted his chin, and lowered his hands. He straightened in his seat, and then flicked an imaginary piece of fluff from his coat. He regarded Bailey for a moment.

'We have a receipt, so you should be talking to McCluskey.'

'Who is McCluskey and where can I find him?' Bailey demanded.

'Duthie will have his details in the file.' Westcott's gaze shifted to the slaughterman. 'Why did you bother me with this matter?'

'He asked for you by name.' Duthie shifted his weight from one foot to the other. 'You're the boss,' he added. 'I only work here.'

'So give him McCluskey's details and get him out of here.' Westcott picked up a paper from his desk and began to scan it.

'Hold your horses,' Bailey cut in. 'You've bought a stolen herd, and if you don't take more interest I'll throw you in jail while I do some checking up. Don't try to give me the run-around around or you'll find yourself holding the dirty end of the stick.'

'You're wasting your time.' Westcott smiled. 'The receipt that McCluskey signed has a disclaimer printed on it which places the responsibility for the legality of the transaction firmly on the seller.'

'Mister, that won't wash with me.' Bailey's patience dissipated. 'If you buy stolen stock then you'll be held responsible. Change your tune or go to jail. That's your choice.'

'There is another option,' Duthie said in a high-pitched tone.

Bailey glanced at the slaughterman and saw him reaching into a pocket of his long white coat, his face contorted with desperation. He began to pull a pistol into view, but the hammer caught in the material of the coat and stopped his action. Bailey grabbed for his gun and it came smoothly out of his holster. He almost lost his balance as the crutch threatened to slide away from him. He reeled as he threw down on Duthie, at the same time being aware that Tim Westcott's right hand was making a quick movement to his left armpit. Then all hell broke loose.

EIGHT

The action occurred in a blur of speed but to Bailey it seemed to unroll slowly. He teetered on the crutch, struggling to maintain his balance. He faced Duthie, who was trying to jerk his pistol clear of his coat pocket, and was aware that Westcott was buying into the shoot-out with a gun from his shoulder holster. Duthie's gun finally pulled clear. Bailey clenched his teeth. It was a life-or-death decision. He was half-facing Duthie so he continued his action against him. He lifted his Colt .45 and snapped a shot at the slaughterman, aiming for the centre of his chest. Gun smoke drifted across the room.

The office rocked with gunfire. Bailey's gun recoiled. He saw Duthie drop his pistol and fall backwards, and turned instantly to face Westcott, who was pulling a short-barrelled pistol into play. Bailey triggered two quick shots across the desk as he sprawled across a corner of it, his crutch flying out of reach. Westcott's gun blasted first, and the bullet broke a pane of glass in the tall window overlooking the street. Bailey's shooting was accurate. His first shot struck Westcott in the stomach and, as he sagged

111

down behind the desk, the second slug hit him in the head. He fell to the floor.

The office door burst open and Cargill came in at a run, gun in hand. He looked around, took in the situation, and nodded before moving back into the doorway to watch the passage outside. The sound of the shots grumbled away. Bailey sat on a corner of the desk, his smoking gun in his hand, and considered the situation. He did not like it. He was being drawn deeper and deeper into this crooked business without getting a grip on the essentials. But he felt he was making some progress. The bad-men were trying to kill him, which proved that he was looking in the right places. He shook his head, dissatisfied with his progress. He needed proof of the guilty, and most of all he wanted Hayman.

Cargill looked in at Bailey from the doorway, grinning. 'Looks like they were guilty sure enough,' he observed. 'Are you OK?'

Bailey nodded. 'Get my crutch, will you? We'd better go to the law office. Lantz will be wondering what's going on. There'll be hell to pay over this when Henry Westcott learns of it.'

'I wonder if he's mixed up in this crooked business,' Cargill observed. 'The Westcott brothers have been running the local cow business for a long time, and they've always been as thick as thieves with the men who are suspected of being on the wrong side of the law.'

'We'll get around to that line of reasoning later.' Bailey stood up. 'Let's go look up McCluskey, whoever he is.' Bailey took the crutch and stuck it under his right arm. He teetered for a moment as he adjusted his balance, and then left the office with Cargill hurrying at his side.

'McCluskey owns a tannery on the outskirts of town,' Cargill volunteered. 'He's always hanging around here. Now we know he brought in your stolen steers we can do something about him. These rustlers must be pretty sure of themselves, using their real names on receipts and the like.'

They left the slaughterhouse and Cargill pushed his way through the crowd that had gathered on the sidewalk, attracted by the shooting. He ignored the questions shouted at him, and Bailey stomped along in silence, his face like stone. Outside the general store, they were confronted by Lantz, whose face showed relief at the sight of them.

'Save it until we get to the office,' Bailey said when the jailer began asking questions.

They continued along the street, and the crowd followed them, calling questions until they entered the law office.

'There'll be hell to pay over this,' Lantz said when he had learned the details of the incident. 'Just wait until Henry Westcott gets word of it. He'll come through Dodge like a blue norther, with his outfit at his back. There'll be gun smoke and lead, and plenty of business for the undertakers. He'll want satisfaction for the death of his brother.'

'We'll cross that bridge when we come to it,' Bailey said. 'He'll know how I feel about my brother when he gets the news. We're going to pick up McCluskey now, and we want Hayman, Gruber's partner. I heard he's the one that killed my brother.'

'You won't find him,' said Lantz, shaking his head. 'I

113

saw him riding out of town earlier, and he looked like he was gonna make a long trip.'

'I'll trail him to Hell and back!' Bailey staggered as he turned to the door, and Lantz put out a steadying hand.

'By the looks of it, you should be resting that leg,' he opined.

'I'll rest up when I've got this crooked business nailed down,' Bailey retorted. 'Are you ready, Cargill?'

Cargill checked his shotgun and then nodded. 'As ready as I'll ever be,' he said.

'Let's visit Henry Westcott before we do anything else,' Bailey decided.

'I was afraid you'd get around to him.' Cargill shook his head. 'Are you sure you wanta tell him you killed his brother?'

'I'll tell him, and I've got some questions to ask him. I know where his office is, so let's go and talk to him.'

There was a crowd on the street, for word of the shooting had got around, and men asked Cargill for information.

'It's to do with the rustling,' Cargill said. 'We're getting to the bottom of it.'

Bailey made for Henry Westcott's office. A young man was seated in the front office, and he shook his head when Bailey asked to see Westcott.

'The boss left town early this morning,' he said. 'He's gone out to his ranch, and won't be back until tomorrow at the earliest.'

'I'll come back tomorrow,' Bailey said. 'In the meantime you better send someone out to Westcott's ranch to tell him his brother has been killed resisting the law.'

Bailey's right leg ached intolerably as they left Wescott's office, and he stifled a groan each time he put his weight on the crutch. He looked around as they headed for the outskirts of Dodge, aware that he had enemies who were complete strangers to him. 'Where does McCluskey hang out, Cargill?' he asked.

'He's got a tannery on the edge of Dodge. It stinks of rawhide, blood, and God knows what else. He's a hard man – a fist-fighter, and hasn't lost a fight around here, which is saying something.'

'Is he law-abiding, do you know?'

'I don't know. You'll get his measure when you speak to him.'

They turned into an alley beyond the livery stable, and came to a rough-looking barn standing alone. Bailey caught a bad smell emanating from the place, and wrinkled his nose. 'We'll make this as short as possible,' he said, and Cargill laughed.

'The shorter the better!' Cargill shifted his shotgun into a more comfortable position.

Bailey stepped into the open doorway and looked around the interior of the barn. It was stiflingly hot, and the stench of blood and rawhide caught at his throat with insidious fingers. He saw two men inside, pawing through a stack of hides, and three women were seated in the background, scraping hides. One of the men looked up, and came immediately towards Bailey, who changed his crutch to his left armpit, eased his weight on to his left side and lifted his right foot off the ground. His right hand dropped to his side close to his holstered gun.

115

'That's McCluskey,' Cargill said in an aside as the man approached.

Bailey studied the big man who came forward aggressively.

'What do you want?' McCluskey demanded.

'You're McCluskey?' Bailey asked.

'That's right.'

'You delivered some steers to Westcott's slaughter house earlier today?'

'Right again.'

'Where did you get them from?'

A shadow appeared in McCluskey's eyes and his shoulders lifted slightly.

'What the hell? How come you're checking into my business? You've got no right to come in here asking questions like that.'

'The cattle were part of a stolen herd, so I've get every right to stick my nose in. Just answer the question, huh?' Bailey was not inclined to give ground.

McCluskey glanced at the law star pinned to Bailey's shirt and shrugged his powerful shoulders. 'I picked them up from Gruber's range,' he grated.

'And was that on Gruber's say-so?'

'You're walking the line, Deputy, so watch your step.' McCluskey considered for a moment, and then said: 'Hell, yes! Gruber asked me to drive them in. Say, are you calling me a rustler?'

Bailey nodded. 'Yes, I am, and I know you're mixed up in the rustling.'

McCluskey stiffened and dropped his hand to his holstered gun. 'You're talking through your hat,' he snarled.

'We've never met before, so you don't know a danged thing about me.'

'We met on the trail outside town last night, and rode out to Gruber's ranch together.' Bailey eyes glinted.

McCluskey moved uneasily. The fingers of his right hand curled around the butt of his holstered pistol.

'I was told that Nick Mason, the rustler, was hiding out in Gruber's line shack,' Bailey continued. 'That's where I saw you, mister, and your name at that time was Mason!'

Cargill brought his shotgun to bear on McCluskey, who half-lifted his pistol from his holster, changed his mind, and thrust it back into leather.

'You're trying to push me into drawing against you,' McCluskey said. He grinned. 'But I'm a little too long in the tooth to fall for that. I don't know who you saw out at Gruber's place but it wasn't me. I was here in Dodge all day and all night, and I can prove it.'

'No doubt you can.' Bailey nodded. 'In fact, I'd be surprised if you didn't have an alibi. But I've got you dead to rights. I saw you in that line shack, and Attree talked to you – called you Mason. So you've got two names you live under – Mason and McCluskey. That's OK. I'm calling you Mason right now, and I'm taking you in for rustling.'

McCluskey made his play without warning. His hand came up filled with a gun, and Bailey, watching intently, set his hand in motion simultaneously. McCluskey was fast, and his gun muzzle swept up. But Bailey had the edge. He drew, cocked the weapon, and fired in a smooth succession of movements. The reports of their guns were like a double knock on a door.

McCluskey's draw ended the instant he squeezed his

trigger. Bailey's slug pierced his heart in the split second before he fired, and he was dead as a reflex action fired his shot. His bullet flew wider; clanged against a metal hinge in the door of the barn behind Bailey. He stood for a moment, his thick legs splayed, and then the life ran out of him and he fell to the ground like a tree uprooted in a hurricane.

Cargill raised his shotgun and covered the other man in the barn, who seemed rooted to the spot in shock; he did not move as Cargill paced forward to arrest him.

Bailey stood motionless, gun in hand, listening to the fading echoes, satisfied that he was dealing with the men directly responsible for the death of his brother, and he was already wondering what he could do next. Gruber was still at liberty, Henry Westcott had to be questioned – arrested if necessary, and Frank Hayman was there in the background. He leaned on the crutch and tried to summon up fresh reserves of strength and determination. He had to see this through to the bitter end.

'This is Pete Whaley,' said Cargill, herding his prisoner forward, a short, fat man who was sweating profusely and looked as if he were on the verge of having a heart attack. 'He says McCluskey is also Nick Mason. I talked to the three women about it and they had nothing to say.'

'Let's take him to jail and talk to him,' Bailey said. 'He'll sing our tune when he finds himself behind bars.'

Cargill menaced Whaley with his shotgun and they made their back towards Main Street, using the alley beside the big saloon. Cargill led the way with the prisoner and Bailey stomped along behind, trying to keep up with them. He found it hard going, and paused to wipe sweat from his face. His leg wound was throbbing, and he thought he should visit the doctor to get it checked. He was hungry, and felt weak inside. He knew he was trying to do too much, but felt that he was winning the fight against the rustlers, and one more good effort might bring about a successful conclusion.

Cargill paused in the alley mouth to check the street, and Bailey caught up with him, unsteady on the crutch and feeling as if he would be unable to take another step. Cargill turned to face him, and then turned his head sharply in a double take to check the street again.

'Hey, there are seven riders just coming into town,' he said. 'They're dismounting outside the livery barn, and one of them is Gruber.'

Bailey pushed forward and looked along the street. He saw the riders, and his eyes glinted when he spotted Gruber addressing the riders. Four of the men turned away immediately and split into two pairs. Bailey watched them striding along the sidewalk; one pair crossed the street to the opposite sidewalk and they continued steadily, obviously searching the buildings fronting the street.

'What do you make of that?' Cargill demanded. 'Are they looking for you?'

'They won't find me in that direction,' Bailey mused.

Gruber made his way to his office along the street, followed by the remaining two men.

'Can you get Whaley into the jail by the back lots?' Bailey asked Cargill.

'Sure I can. It'll be no trouble at all. What are you going to do?'

'I'll stick around here and keep an eye on Gruber, and pick him up if I get the chance.'

'Do you want me to come back here when I've dropped off the prisoner?'

'No. You'd better stick around the jail. I can manage on my own.'

Cargill went back along the alley with the prisoner, and turned to the right when he reached the back lots. Bailey, watching Gruber, saw him pause outside his office with the two bodyguards in close attendance. They chatted for a moment, and then the two men left Gruber and came along the street in Bailey's direction. Gruber went into his office. Bailey turned instantly, went back along the alley, and crossed the back lots to the alley beside Gruber's office.

He went to the alley mouth and glanced around the street. There was no sign of Gruber's gun men. He eased his pistol in its holster, left the alley, and entered Gruber's office. Gruber was on one knee in front of a small safe in a corner, removing papers and money. His fleshy face changed expression when he saw Bailey. He reached into the safe and picked up a gun. Bailey drew his pistol and cocked it.

'Drop your gun or I'll kill you,' he said.

Gruber paused, and then dropped the gun. He got to his feet slowly and raised his hands. 'Where in hell did you come from?' he demanded. 'I thought I'd got rid of you. Where's Waco and Donovan?'

'They're dead, and I've come for you.'

Gruber grinned. 'I've got six men in town with me,' he said. 'You won't get far.'

'I'm not going far. We'll take a walk along the back lots to the jail, and I'll put you in a cell. Come on. Don't try to get smart or you'll wind up dead before your time. You've got a lot to answer for, Gruber – and so has Hayman. Where has he gone? I heard he rode out earlier.'

'Hayman's gone?' Gruber shook his head. 'So that's where the money in the safe has gone. He's turned yellow and run.'

'He's got more sense than you. He's still loose, but you've come to the end of your rope, Gruber.'

Gruber moistened his lips as he glanced around his office. Then he sighed and shook his head. He looked at the steady pistol in Bailey's hand, shrugged, and headed for the door.

'Not so fast,' Bailey warned him as they entered the alley, and Gruber slowed his pace. When they reached the back lots they headed for the rear of the law office, sticking close to the buildings fronting Main Street.

Bailey hammered on the back door of the jail, and several moments passed before the door creaked open and Cargill's face appeared in the doorway. He grinned when he saw Gruber, and took him into a cell.

'Search him,' Bailey said, and stood by while Cargill did so.

'I want to see my lawyer,' Gruber said. 'He'll soon have me out of here.'

'He won't; he's on a trip to Abilene, so Lantz told me,' Cargill said. 'He won't be back for a week at least.'

Bailey looked into the cell where Buck Stanton was lying on a bunk. The deputy was conscious, and he nodded at Bailey.

'How are you doing, Buck?' Bailey asked.

'Doc tells me I should make it,' Stanton said slowly. 'Are you making any progress?'

'We're getting to it.'

'I sure wish I was able to do my job,' Stanton said.

Bailey sat down on the end of the bunk and stretched his right leg out, sighing with relief as he did so. He explained his experiences since pinning on the law badge, and saw shock spread across Stanton's pale features.

'Hell, I reckon you've just about cleaned up around here,' Stanton mused.

'There are a few more points to be cleared up,' Bailey replied.

'You'd better tell Cargill to get a posse together and keep them around the jail for a few days, until you've done what you think has got to be done. If gunmen come in from Gruber's ranch they'll take over the town, and any witnesses you have will disappear. Don't waste time, Bailey. You need some strong backing. Where is Cargill? I'll give him some orders.'

'I'm right here, Buck,' Cargill said from the door. 'What do you want?'

'I'm gonna visit the doc,' Bailey said, 'and then I'm gonna get me some grub.'

'You'd better stay here,' Stanton said. 'Don't take any chances. Call the doc in, and have a meal delivered from the diner. You're right up against it now.'

'Gruber's brought in half a dozen hardcases,' Cargill said. 'They're wandering around the street right now. I'll sneak out the back door and gather the posse. I'll call in the doc, Bailey, and then organize some food.'

'OK!' Bailey nodded. 'I'm feeling kinda played out. I need to rest up. I'll stay in the office and watch for trouble.'

He limped through to the front office and eased himself into the seat behind the desk. His shoulders sagged and he struggled against the weakness that flowed through his body. He drew his gun and checked it, reloaded empty chambers, and placed the weapon on the desk where he could reach it easily. It was all he could do to prepare himself for any action that might come from the bad-men.

When Doc Alwyn came into the office, carrying his medical bag, Bailey reached for his gun. The doctor closed the door, and turning, looked down the barrel of the weapon.

'Expecting trouble?' Alwyn demanded.

'I'm not taking any chances,' Bailey replied. 'Take a look at my leg, Doc. It's giving me hell.'

'I expect you've ignored my instructions.'

'Not from choice.' Bailey grimaced.

The doctor attended to his leg, and Bailey bore the ministrations without complaint. 'The wound is inflamed,' Alwyn commented. 'You could have trouble with it if you persist in ignoring my instructions.'

'I'll do what I have to, and then settle down to rest. It's the best I can do under the circumstances.'

'Sure. I just want you to know the risks you're running by stomping around on it.'

'It's feeling easier already,' Bailey said when the doctor had bandaged the wound.

Alwyn departed. Bailey passed the time cleaning his

gun, and was reloading it when the street door was opened and Stella Pearson came into the office. She smiled at him and turned to close the door, but was sent flying off balance as someone behind her thrust the door inward. Stella fell to the floor with a cry of pain. Bailey cocked his gun when he saw two of Gruber's bad-men lunging in through the doorway. . . .

NINE

Bailey saw the foremost intruder trip on the threshold, fall to his hands and knees and drop his pistol. The second man lunged to his left as he entered, and lifted his gun to start shooting. Bailey squeezed his trigger and filled the office with gun thunder. Smoke swirled, and his bullet slammed into the bad-man, knocking him sideways. The other man scrabbled for his gun, found it, and then looked up into the muzzle of Bailey's levelled gun. He threw down his weapon as if it had become suddenly too hot to hold.

Bailey got to his feet and leaned his left hand on the desk, his pistol covering the man at the door. His ears were protesting at the noise of the shooting, his throat was irritated by the gun smoke. He glanced at Stella, who was sitting on the floor in the corner where she had been pushed.

'Are you hurt?' he asked.

She got to her feet, rubbing an elbow. Her face was pale, but she forced a smile. 'I'm OK,' she said, coming to

125

the desk and sitting on a chair.

The street door was thrust open and Cargill stepped in over the threshold, his shotgun ready in his hands. He covered the prisoner with the gun.

'Are you all right, Bailey?' he demanded.

'Yeah.' Bailey sat down again and eased his leg. 'These two came busting in. They're Gruber's men. I recognize the one wearing the red shirt. I reckon we should go out and confront the other four before they get wise and come shooting.'

'I'll stick this one in the cells.' Cargill motioned to the gunman. 'Empty your pockets on the desk. What's your name?'

'I don't have one.'

'You'll have one before we finish with you. You ride for Gruber, huh?'

'I ain't saying.'

Cargill picked up the cell keys. He pushed the prisoner towards the door leading into the cell block and followed him closely. Bailey shook his head, wondering what would happen next. The street door opened again at that moment, and Bailey's gun leapt into his hand. He covered the man who entered, and grimaced when he recognized Henry Westcott. The cattle buyer was wearing a cartridge belt and holstered gun. He had evidently heard the news about his brother's death for his face was lined with grief; his eyes hard and over-bright. He stepped around the dead man of the floor with hardly a glance at him and came to the desk.

'You killed my brother, Bailey,' he said, his voice flat and toneless. 'What happened?'

126

'It was self-defence,' Bailey responded. 'I intended arresting him on a charge of handling rustled cattle. His slaughterman, Duthie, pulled a gun, and your brother reached for his gun in a shoulder holster. I shot Duthie. Your brother pulled his gun, and I waited until the last possible moment before shooting him. He would have killed me if I'd held my fire.'

Westcott nodded slowly. He looked at the law star on Bailey's shirtfront. Bailey watched him closely, fearing he might draw his gun to avenge his brother's death. But Westcott kept his hand away from his gun butt.

'So what happened?' Westcott demanded. 'You found your stolen stock out on the range, huh? Did you trail them into my brother's yard?'

'I did, but that was only a part of it. The herd had been split. One part came here to be slaughtered, and the rest was on Gruber's ranch.' Bailey described the events that led to Cargill saving his life.

'So Gruber is a part of this.' Westcott shook his head sadly.

'Didn't you know?' Bailey countered.

'Do you think I'm mixed up in this crooked business?'

'I have to ask questions to get at the truth.'

'I have nothing to do with the crookedness around here. Check me out.'

'I'll do that. Gruber is behind bars, and he'll be charged with attempting to murder me. I'm sorry I had to shoot your brother, Westcott.'

Westcott sighed and turned away. He departed silently, his shoulders bowed and his eyes downcast. Bailey heaved a sigh as the street door closed behind him. He looked at

Stella, who began to speak, but Cargill returned from the cell block and dumped the bunch of keys on a corner of the desk.

'What are we going to do about the rest of Gruber's men?' he demanded.

'Pick them up. Are you ready?'

Cargill grinned and drew his pistol, checked it and returned it to his holster. He broke his shotgun, checked that both barrels were loaded, and closed it again.

'I'm loaded for bear,' he said. 'Are you up to hunting through the town?'

'Yes, but I want to talk to Stella first,' Bailey responded.

Cargill nodded. 'Stanton is sitting up in his cell. I gave him a pistol, and he'll guard the prisoners until we get back. I'll lock the street door when we leave. I'll be outside, watching the street, until you're ready to go.'

Bailey turned his attention to the silent Stella as Cargill left the office.

'Sorry about what's happening,' he said. 'We're up to our necks in it this morning. How can I help you?'

'I just wanted to see how you were doing,' she replied.

'I'm OK, thanks.' Bailey got to his feet and tucked the crutch under his right arm. 'I'll escort you back to the store. You shouldn't be out alone. It isn't safe yet.'

'I won't venture out again,' she said, looking troubled. 'It's good that you've put Gruber in jail, but his men are still around, and they want our ranch. Dad and I are in big trouble while they are on the loose. Come and see me at the store if you get time, and take care of your leg. You'll be sorry if it turns bad.'

He nodded. 'Thanks for the advice. I'm sorry to hurry

you but I've got a lot to do.'

They left the office. The sun was low in the west and shadows were creeping into the corners. Bailey looked around the street. It seemed peaceful enough, and he wondered why nobody had come to investigate the shooting. Cargill locked the office and they went along the street to the store.

As they neared the doorway of the general store two of the men who had accompanied Gruber into town emerged. One was filling his cartridge belt with shells from a box of .45 shells he had just bought. The other looked around, and reached for his holstered gun when he saw Bailey and Cargill together only yards away. He shouted a warning to his companion, who ceased his reloading and closed the gun.

Bailey reached out and pushed Stella towards the alley beside the store; she hurried into cover. Bailey dropped the crutch when he made his draw, and tottered as his gun came to hand. He took a step to his left to maintain his balance, cursing the pain that shafted through his leg. But he concentrated on his draw, and cocked his gun as the foresight covered the nearest man. Then Cargill's shotgun blasted, and the whirling load of 12-gauge pellets hit the gun man squarely in the chest. He was hurled backwards by the impact, and fell to the sidewalk with a three-inch hole in his heart and his blood spurting.

The other man dropped his gun before Bailey could shoot him and lifted his hands.

'Jail him, Cargill,' Bailey said. 'I'll wait in the store. We could do with a couple of your posse men backing us.'

'They'll be turning up at the jail at any time now,'

Cargill replied. 'I'll tell Lantz to send a couple of them to join us. We need to get this man-hunting over before sundown.'

Bailey escorted Stella into the store. There was fear in her eyes when she looked at him. He patted her shoulder.

'Don't worry. I'll see you later,' he said, and went out to the sidewalk.

'Have you found out yet who shot your brother?' she called.

Bailey paused and pivoted on the crutch. His face looked as if it had been carved from stone. His eyes glinted. He grimaced and then shrugged.

'I've got a name,' he told her, 'but I'll have to let it rest there until I can find the time to handle it.'

'And what will you do when this is over?' she persisted.

Bailey sighed and shook his head. 'I can't think that far ahead. I can't walk out of this. I've got to see it through. There'll be time to worry about the future when it arrives.'

There were a couple of chairs on the sidewalk outside the store and Bailey sat down thankfully. Stella came to stand beside him.

'No,' he said quickly. 'Don't stand there. Gruber brought six gun men into town a short while ago. We've got four of them, so two more are still loose, and they'll shoot on sight. Go in now, and stay away from the windows.'

'Take care,' she said, and stepped back into the store.

Bailey watched the street. Life was going on as usual, he noticed – but not for him. He considered the incidents that had overtaken him since Thad died and the herd was stolen. Who would have suspected that such large-scale crookedness had been going on under cover in this community? The bad-men had everything going their way, and it was no wonder that the sheriff had been killed recently in the execution of his duty.

Presently Cargill reappeared on the sidewalk and came swiftly to where Bailey was seated. His shotgun was tucked under his arm, and his eyes constantly studied his surroundings. Bailey pushed himself to his feet and leaned on the crutch. He wouldn't be sorry when this business had been settled.

'Lantz is helping Stanton to interrogate the prisoners,' Cargill said, 'but they ain't having much luck. Gruber is up on his high horse, demanding to be turned loose. Hooton, the saloon man, says he's innocent and there'll be trouble for the law department when he can get hold of a lawyer. Nobody is saying anything worth a damn. It all started when your herd was rustled, and you'd think, to hear the talk going on, that the cows stole themselves.'

'It'll all come out in the wash,' Bailey mused. 'We'd better get on and find the other two men who came into town with Gruber. I'll know them by sight. The sooner we get them the better. Have you any idea where they might be?'

'One of them is Joe Catton, who is friendly with Widow Parker. She runs a guest house on South Street. Catton was heading in that direction when we saw him – him and Frank Smith. It might pay us to drop in there and look around.'

'Lead the way.' Bailey steeled his weary body to continue.

Cargill crossed the street and entered an alley. Bailey gritted his teeth as he plodded on. They reached the

131

intersection where South Street crossed Main Street, and Bailey saw several rows of buildings stretching away to the south. Cargill led the way to a large two-storey property with a sign out front bearing the legend: JANE PARKER – GUEST HOUSE.

'Catton might be inside,' Cargill said.

'I'm hoping he is,' Bailey responded.

Cargill reached the doorr and rapped on the centre panel. Bailey caught up with him as the door was opened and a tall, slender woman appeared. She was wearing a blue dress with a white collar, and looked neat and cool. Her blue eyes sparkled when she recognized Cargill.

'Good morning, Mr Cargill,' she greeted. 'How can I help you?'

Bailey moved forward impatiently, and she peered at him, her expression changing.

'Has there been an accident?' she demanded.

'He was shot, and it was no accident,' Cargill replied. 'We're looking for Joe Catton. I saw him on Main Street a short time ago, heading in this direction. Have you seen him?'

'Is he in some kind of trouble?' she asked.

'I don't think so,' Bailey said before Cargill could reply. 'I'd like to ask him some questions. It's possible that he can help the law.'

A door banged violently somewhere inside the house, and heavy footsteps sounded.

'He's inside,' Bailey said sharply.

'And it sounds like he's making a run for the back door,' Cargill replied.

He pushed Mrs Parker aside and ran into the house.

Bailey turned and moved as fast as the crutch would permit. He went to the side of the house, turned the corner, and hurried to the rear. He heard the boom of Cargill's shotgun, and a pistol was fired in response. When he reached the rear corner and peered around it he saw Cargill standing over a prone figure.

'He ain't hurt,' Cargill said. 'I fired the shotgun into the air, and he fired a shot before throwing down his gun. This is Joe Catton, Bailey, and he should be able to help us in our enquiries.'

'It's about time we started taking prisoners,' Bailey remarked. 'We need to talk to some of these guys to find out what's going on.'

Cargill ordered Catton to his feet. He was not young: early forties, a tall, lean man with piercing blue eyes.

'Why are you chasing me?' he demanded truculently.

'Because you were running away from the house,' Cargill said with a grin. 'We wanted to talk to you, is all, and you acted like a runaway bull. I reckon you've got a guilty conscience, so we'll take you in and ask some questions. Where's Frank Smith?'

'I ain't his keeper. If you want him you'll have to find him.'

'We'll surely do that.' Cargill prodded him with the muzzle of the shotgun.

'You take him in,' Bailey said to Cargill. 'I can't keep up with you. I'll check out the saloon for Smith.'

'I'll meet you there,' Cargill replied.

Bailey slowed his pace. He needed to rest, take the weight off his injured leg and give it time to heal. But while Thad's killer was on the loose he would force himself to keep going. The shadows were deepening. Lights were beginning to glimmer in some windows. He reached Main Street and crossed to the big saloon, which was open despite the fact that Hooton, the saloon man, was in jail. He entered and paused on the threshold to look around. There was a different bartender, and almost a dozen men inside. Bailey checked over the men and saw that one of them was the man who had accompanied Gruber into town. Frank Smith, he decided, and stomped along the bar until he was standing behind him. He leaned his weight on his left side and grasped the butt of his pistol.

'Frank Smith,' he said quietly, and the man looked over his shoulder.

Smith was short and fleshy; dressed in range clothes, and looked like a cowboy although he had the hard-bitten look of a gunhand. His narrowed brown eyes studied Bailey's face for a moment, and then his gaze dropped to the crutch.

'Is this some kind of a joke?' he demanded.

'Not from where I'm standing,' Bailey replied. 'Are you Frank Smith?'

'That's my business. What's it to you?'

'You ride for Gruber, huh?'

'He pays my wages,' Smith conceded.

'Then put your hands up and I'll have your gun. I'm gonna take you to the law office. You'll be questioned.'

'The hell you will!' Smith stepped to his left and put space between them.

'Don't do anything stupid,' Bailey warned.

'What do you want to question me about? I don't

know a thing.'

'Let's go along to the law office. I'll take your gun.'

'Why do you need to take my gun? Am I under arrest?'

'I'm taking you in for questioning. If you've done nothing wrong then you've got nothing to fear.'

Smith edged his right hand towards the butt of his gun. Bailey prepared himself for action.

'If you look like you're gonna draw your gun I'll have no option but to draw and shoot,' Bailey said.

Smith studied his face for some moments, and then heaved a sigh and raised his hands.

'Take the gun,' he said. 'You ain't gonna back down, and I ain't about to risk my life for a few questions.'

Bailey sighed in relief and drew Smith's gun from its holster. They left the saloon. Bailey stomped along on his crutch, holding Smith's gun in his left hand. Cargill appeared on the boardwalk, shotgun under his right arm, and came up to take charge of Smith.

'You should heed the doc's instructions and take some time off,' Cargill observed. 'You look like you're on your last legs. If you were my hoss I'd shoot you to put you out of your misery.'

'I've a mind to take things easy for a spell,' Bailey replied. 'There are several things I need to check on, and there's no time like the present. Tell Stanton I'll see him in the morning. We've cleaned up around here considerable.'

'There'll be at least six posse men in the office shortly,' Cargill observed, 'all wearing special deputy badges, and they'll be around for as long as they are needed. You better watch out around town though. You've got to be ready for trouble to jump out at you when you least expect it.'

'I'm on my guard. I'll see you around, Cargill. We've done pretty well together.'

Cargill grinned and went back along the sidewalk preceded by Smith. Bailey watched their progress for a moment, and then heaved a sigh and turned to survey the street. Frank Hayman was uppermost in his mind, and he looked at the land office while he wondered where the alleged killer of his brother had gone. He went to the office and entered to confront a young man seated at a desk.

'Mr Gruber ain't in the office right now,' the clerk said, 'and I'm about finished for the day.' His blue eyes shone with honesty. He was smartly dressed in a grey store suit, looked clean and neat, and he was lean, good-looking and mentally bright. 'Gruber won't be back for several days.'

'I think he'll be away a lot longer than that,' Bailey said. 'But I'm more interested in Frank Hayman right now. Where will I find him?'

'He's gone out on business – left town on his horse about noon. I don't know when he'll get back. He's always close-mouthed about his movements.'

Bailey nodded. He pulled forward a chair and sat down at the desk opposite the clerk; leaned his crutch against the desk.

'What's your name?' he asked.

'Dick Coe, sir.'

'You handle all the office paperwork?'

'Sure. That's my job.'

'What can you tell me about the Pearson ranch?'

136

'I can't discuss business. It would be more than my job is worth.'

'As I see it, your job has reached the end of its trail. I arrested Gruber, Hayman has hit the trail and I doubt if he'll come back, and that's why I'm here. Gruber has been buying up small ranches, using threats to persuade the owners to sell out. I was out at the Pearson ranch when Gruber and Hayman showed up there with a gunhand, who was killed. You must know what was going on, so tell me about it.'

Coe eyed the law star on Bailey's shirt front. He shook his head. 'It looks like I could be in a lot of trouble,' he mused.

'I was about to tell you that. But if you went along to the law office now and made a voluntary statement about what was going on in this business, then you could get yourself off the hook. Think it over.'

'I will.' Coe nodded. 'Hayman talked to me before he pulled out – said he'd be back in about a week. I don't think he was involved Mr Gruber's crooked business.'

'He was with Gruber when Mike Pearson was shot so I'd think there's a pretty good chance that he was involved. But you want to think about your place in this, and you need to get your story straight before Hayman returns, if he ever does.' Bailey got to his feet and tucked the crutch under his right arm. He looked down at Coe. 'Does Hayman have a family? Where does he live?'

'He's a loner. There's no woman in his life. He rents a room in Widow Parker's guest house. She'll know about him, if anyone does.'

'Widow Parker's guest house, huh? That's interesting.

Don't forget what I told you about reporting to the law office.'

Bailey departed, walked to South Street through the growing darkness, and knocked on the door of the guest house. Mrs Parker answered, and her smile of welcome vanished when she recognized him.

'I'm sorry about the trouble we had here earlier,' he said, 'and I hope this visit will pass without incident. I'm interested in Frank Hayman this time. I understand that he's left Dodge, heading east. Did he tell you where he was going and for how long?'

'I saw him at breakfast and he mentioned he was riding out at noon. But he didn't say anything about the trip.'

'Did he say he would return?'

'Not a word. But he goes away often and always returns. I took it for granted that he intended coming back because I'm sure he would have told me if he had other plans.'

'Can you tell me anything about his movements? For instance, was he here on the night of the storm? Did he stay in or was he out?'

'I don't know. There's no way I would check up on a guest's movements. What is this about?'

'I'd like to take a look in Hayman's room. We have to eliminate him from an event that happened recently.'

'And you expect to find evidence in his room?' She shook her head. 'I don't think I can do that, even for the law.'

'It would save us all a lot of trouble if you agreed,' Bailey persisted. 'If I had to see the judge for a warrant there might be some publicity that would not help your business. I am making an investigation into criminal activity in and around Dodge City, and at the moment Hayman is under suspicion. The fact that he has gone away looks bad for him.'

'If you put it like that then I could unlock his door and let you look inside. You'd better come in.'

Bailey suppressed a sigh and entered. He had some trouble mounting the stairs, and his injured leg was throbbing by the time they entered Hayman's room. It was sparsely furnished – a single bed, a cabinet beside the bed, and a wardrobe. There were no personal items lying around to indicate that the room was occupied. Bailey crossed to the wardrobe and opened the door. It was empty except for a pile of range clothes lying on the floor inside.

He checked the clothes – a pair of denim pants, a pale-blue shirt, a neckerchief and a leather vest. The clothes were damp, and Bailey recalled the slashing rain of that stormy night when his herd was stolen.

'Thank you, Mrs Parker,' he said, returning the clothes to the wardrobe. 'Perhaps you'll inform the law office when Hayman comes back.'

He left the guest house and paused to consider. He needed a witness who had seen Hayman out riding that night with Gruber's men, and wondered if the liveryman had seen Hayman leave town. He made his way back to Main Street and headed for the livery barn.

When he entered the barn he heard loud voices coming from the small office, and as he limped across he heard the sound of a blow and a cry of pain. He drew his pistol, moved into the office doorway, and saw Pete McKay lying on the floor in front of his desk. Two men were standing over him – one holding a gun.

'Get up and take what's coming to you,' one of the men was saying.

'What's going on?' Bailey demanded.

The man with the gun swung around to face the door, lifting his gun to cover Bailey, who squeezed his trigger. The office was rocked by the shot. Bailey's slug struck the gun man in the left thigh and he fell down. The second man reached for his holstered gun.

'Don't try it,' warned Bailey, and the man froze. 'So what gives?' Bailey continued.

McKay scrambled to his feet. His right eye was swollen and blood stained his cheek. He snatched the gun out of the holster of the second man and backed off with it, looking as if he would start shooting.

'Hold it,' Bailey said. 'Don't shoot him. I need to ask him some questions and get some answers.'

'He's Zeke Caulfield,' McKay said, 'one of Henry Westcott's crew. Him and Sol Mathew came in throwing their weight about and attacked me. They warned me not to talk to the law about what's going on around here.'

'Do you know what's going on?' Bailey asked.

'I do get to see a lot that normal folk don't,' said McKay, shrugging. 'I'm here day and night, and I see everyone that rides in or leaves town. But I don't talk about what I see.'

'What's Henry Westcott doing that he's afraid someone will talk about it?'

'I got nothing to say.' McKay shook his head stubbornly.

'Did you see Hayman ride out of town on the night of

140

the storm?' Bailey asked.

'Why don't you take this hardcase to the jail, lock him up, and then come back to talk to me?' Mackay suggested. 'I might remember something by then.'

'OK. I'll do that.' Bailey motioned with his pistol and the hardcase started for the door. 'Hold it,' Bailey continued. 'We'll take your pard with us. Get him up and help him.'

The wounded man was lifted to his feet and walked out of the office. His left leg was bleeding badly, and he complained, but Bailey forced them to keep moving and they headed for the jail.

The law office was crowded with men, it seemed, when Bailey entered behind his two prisoners. The posse men had turned up, and Lantz was arranging duties for them. Bailey saw his prisoners locked behind bars and gave Lantz details of the incident.

'Stanton wants you to make a report on all the shooting today,' Lantz said.

'That will have to wait,' Bailey said. 'I'm chasing up one or two things, and I'll let Buck know about them in good time. Right now I'm going back to the stable to talk to McKay. I think he'll be able to tell me a lot about what's been going on around here.'

He departed and stomped along the sidewalk, eager to learn what he could about the crookedness that had flourished in Dodge. Shadows were heavy when he entered the stable.

A lantern was burning feebly, suspended from a beam, As he crossed to the office, a shot crashed somewhere inside, sending shock waves through the building. When he realized that he was not the target he drew his gun and hurried forward, fearing the worst, to find Pete Mackay stretched out in the office with a bullet hole in his forehead.

TEN

Bailey looked around quickly, gun in hand, expecting to find the killer close by, but there was no sign of anyone. A window that looked out into an alley had one broken pane of glass, and he guessed the shot had been fired from there. He could hear running footsteps receding along the alley, and shook his head as he looked down at the dead liveryman. He moved out of the office, looking around for trouble. The interior of the barn was gloomy, and there was no movement anywhere except for horses kicking and chafing in their stalls.

A six-gun blasted in the rear of the building, by the big back door that gave access to corrals out back. The bullet smacked into the door of the office, missing Bailey by a scant inch. He ducked and drew his gun. A second gun threw a string of four shots in quick succession from the front doorway, and Bailey realized that he would have been hit if he had not moved quickly.

He fired at the figure in the front doorway, and jarred his injured leg when he moved on. His shot caused the man to duck back out of sight, and Bailey paused and waited for him to reappear. He came forward again, lifting his gun, and Bailey snapped a shot at him, which struck him high in the body and tumbled him to the ground.

Bailey limped to his left, and the gun at the rear of the stable blasted again. He heard a slug bore through the woodwork of the nearest stall, and a horse inside jumped and began to kick frenziedly. The animal fell to the ground and quivered for a moment before relaxing. Hot lead screeched across the barn. Bailey dropped his crutch, went to ground, and worked his gun until the hammer fell upon an empty chamber. He reloaded quickly.

Silence came and gun echoes faded. Bailey eased his position and looked around. He could see no one. Then a voice called:

'You're pinned down, Bailey. I've got six men around you, and if you don't come out within two minutes I'll send them in after you.'

Bailey heard the ultimatum but did not recognize the voice.

'Who in hell are you?' he demanded.

'Henry Westcott. You didn't think I'd let you get away with killing my brother, did you? Come on out and I'll give you an even break.'

'I'll come out alone and you'll have six gunnies backing you.' Bailey laughed harshly. 'That doesn't sound like an even break – more like murder.'

'The choice is yours. I'm waiting on you.'

'This has got nothing to do with your brother's death. It's obvious that you're mixed up in the big steal that's going on around here, and I'm the only one who's picked up on it. Bring the truth out into the open, Westcott, and then I'll face you. Don't hide behind your brother.'

The silence deepened as tense moments flitted by. The shooting began again, heavier now, and Bailey guessed the gunmen were coming for him. Some came in at the big front door and others joined Westcott at the rear. The barn shook to heavy detonations. Bailey ducked lead and stayed low.

He felt a bullet burn his right forearm below the elbow. He dropped his pistol, and scrabbled for it on the straw-strewn ground. His Stetson was jerked from his head as if an invisible hand had snatched at it. His right leg jerked when a slug ricocheted off a metal harness near by and struck his boot. He stayed low and reloaded his empty cylinder, teeth clenched, eyes watching his surroundings.

When the shooting slackened Bailey eased up into a firing position and looked for targets. He saw a man sneaking along the aisle that cut through the barn from front to back; moving like a shadow from stall to stall, pistol upraised in his right fist and watching for movement. The shooting recommenced, and Bailey fired a single shot at the man he could see as he dropped back into cover. The man dropped his gun and followed it to the ground.

Bailey knew he could not win this fight against superior numbers, but he was unable to disengage. They had him cornered, and it would be only a matter of time before their weight of fire wore him down. He watched for Westcott, feeling that if he could nail him then the gunmen might pull out. It looked like the only chance he had.

He crawled into an empty stall, ready to sell his life dearly. The degree of shooting increased considerably; raking the interior of the barn with flying lead. He heard

145

a voice yelling insistently, trying to make itself heard above the shooting. An uncertain silence fell as men paused in their grim work to hear what was being said.

'Stop the shooting. This is a lawful posse, so come out of the barn and throw down your guns.'

Bailey recognized Cargill's voice and a thrill of relief seeped into his mind.

'Cargill,' he called. 'This is Bailey. Henry Westcott has got me pinned down in here. He means to kill me for shooting his brother.'

Westcott's voice rang out in reply. 'Get out of there, men, and head back to the ranch. I'll finish this off personally.'

Bailey's ears were throbbing from the volume of fire that had been tossed at him. He sagged into cover and remained motionless until Cargill's voice came again.

'OK, you can come on out now, Bailey. They've gone.'

Bailey got to his to his feet and picked up the crutch. He holstered his gun and limped to where Cargill was standing near the front door, flanked by three posse men. 'I guessed it was you in trouble,' Cargill said.

'Mackay is dead in his office,' Bailey countered. 'I don't know who killed him, but Westcott's men were around the barn at the time.'

'We'll pick up Westcott.' Cargill was in command of the situation. 'I thought you were resting up.'

'I'll do that now, if I get the chance. I'll take a room at the hotel.'

'I'll walk with you,' Cargill said. 'Willard, take over here while I'm gone. I'll be back shortly.'

Bailey was relieved when he left the barn. He watched

his surroundings as they walked along the sidewalk. Cargill accompanied him to the door of the hotel and then turned back.

'See you tomorrow,' the posse man said as he returned to the livery barn.

Bailey entered the hotel, rented a room, took his key, and went up to his room. He was exhausted. He entered the room and locked the door. Removing his gunbelt, he dropped on to the bed and closed his eyes. Despite his pain, he fell asleep almost immediately and sank into blessed oblivion.

He awoke stiff and filled with pain, his body demanding more sleep. He lifted his head and looked around wondering what had disturbed him, and heard knocking on the door. He stifled a yawn and pushed his body off the bed, paused to draw his pistol from its holster, and then unlocked the door. Cargill stood outside, clutching his shotgun.

'Did I wake you?'

'What do you think? What's the time?'

'I left you outside this place at nine last evening and it's now eleven the next morning. I'm sorry to disturb you, Bailey, but I thought you ought to know that Stella Pearson is gonna take her father back to their place this afternoon. I don't think she should do that because this business ain't settled yet, but she won't take my advice. You might be able to make her listen to good sense.'

'I'll surely try!' Bailey buckled his gunbelt around his waist and holstered his gun. 'I'll talk to her now.' He stuck the crutch into his right armpit and they descended the stairs. Bailey stifled a yawn. He could have down with several more hours asleep.

'I didn't arrest Westcott last night,' Cargill said. 'He pulled out with his men before we could get him. A posse has gone out to his ranch this morning to pick him up. I'm acting as deputy until things quieten down again. Gruber has been charged with attempting to murder you, with rustling thrown in, and Stanton wants a statement from you to make the charge stick. We're getting on top of this trouble now, thanks to you.'

Bailey nodded. 'I'll get some grub, see Stella, and then drop into the office. If you're doing the deputy's job then I'll take a back seat. I need some time to myself.'

They parted outside the hotel. Bailey went to the diner and had a meal. Afterwards he felt better fitted to face the day, and went along to the general store to see Stella. As he stomped along the sidewalk he was relieved that the pain in his leg wound had eased.

He entered the store. Stella emerged from behind the counter and came to him. Her face had lost some of its worry and, as she smiled, he noticed that she was beautiful. He drew a deep breath, glad that he had been able to help her.

'How's your leg this morning?' she asked.

'It's much better, thanks.'

'I was at the law office earlier to see you and they told me you had gone off duty. I was hoping to see you again because I'm taking my dad back to the ranch.'

'Cargill told me about that. I thought your dad was too ill to be moved.'

'He's feeling much better, and can't wait to get back home. He's afraid someone will move in out there if the place is left unoccupied.'

148

'I wouldn't let that happen.' He looked into her blue eyes and could see his reflection in their pale depths. A remote thought flitted through his mind – he would never see her again if he pulled out for California when this trouble was at an end. 'I don't think you should leave town at this time, Stella. You wouldn't be safe on the ranch with no protection.'

'I think the trouble is over now. You took care of it.'

'It isn't finished. This is just a lull. There are bad-men still operating, and they'll come back when you least expect them.'

'It's not my decision. Dad wants to go back home, and he'll get better much faster there than here in town. Gruber was the cause of our trouble and he's behind bars, where he ought to be.'

Bailey could tell that her mind was made up and did not push the point. He nodded and turned away.

'I'll drop by the ranch when I get the time and see how you're doing.'

She grasped his arm and halted him, her face suddenly anxious again. 'I was thinking that you need to rest your leg and you could come to the ranch and spend a few days with us. We owe you a lot, and this way we could repay it.'

'That's good of you.' He smiled. 'I'll think about it. What time are you leaving?'

'Dad says early this afternoon.'

'I'll come and see you before you go. Right now I have to go to the law office and make a statement on what happened yesterday.'

'I hope you'll be able to come with us,' she said, half-pleading and, when he left her, she stood in the doorway

149

of the store to watch his progress along the street.

Bailey was pleased with her invitation. He had already decided to follow her wagon when it left and watch the ranch, unknown to her, for a few days in case of trouble. But he liked the thought of openly spending time in her company. He had to wait for Hayman to return to Dodge, and had no intention of quitting before he killed the man who murdered his brother.

He went to the law office and found Stanton propped up in a chair at the desk. The deputy was heavily bandaged around the chest. His face was pale, gaunt, his eyes dark-circled and over-bright. He grinned wanly at Bailey's appearance.

'How's the leg?' Stanton demanded.

'Not so painful this morning. How are you doing?'

'I wouldn't be sitting here if it wasn't urgent. You sure put it over on Gruber. I want a statement that he ordered your death so I can charge him officially, and I need a report on all the deaths that have occurred. Cargill told me most of it, but I want it down on paper. And Henry Westcott! Did you get the lowdown on him? Is he mixed up in what's been going on? Was he in with his brother Tim?'

'I didn't get any evidence of that, but he certainly tried to kill me in the livery barn last sight because I shot his brother.'

'It'll all come out when we question the men already behind bars.' Stanton spoke confidently. 'Someone will talk. They always do.'

'I'll write the reports now,' Bailey said. 'Stella and her dad are going back to their ranch this afternoon, and I reckon to go with them. I want to rest my leg now, and they need some protection. They won't be safe until Hayman is behind bars.'

'That's a good idea.' Stanton nodded. 'It's the best thing you can do.'

Bailey pulled a chair to the table. He settled down to writing reports, reliving the grim incidents of the previous day as he recounted them. The rest of the morning passed before he finished the task, and he was telling Stanton the background to the shooting of Gruber's gunmen when Stella entered the office.

'I'm ready to leave with my dad,' she said. 'Are you coming with us?'

'Yes.' Bailey nodded. 'I want to be around if any of the men we haven't arrested show up. The bad-men certainly wanted to get their hands on your ranch, and they may decide to strike again when they learn that you've returned home.'

She suppressed a shudder. 'I sincerely hope they won't,' she said nervously. 'I thought that with Gruber in jail all our troubles would be over.'

'I'll be there to help out if there is any trouble,' he assured her. 'I'll collect my horse from the barn. Where's your wagon?'

'It's outside the store. You can tie your horse behind and ride in the wagon. It'll be easier on your leg.'

Bailey nodded. They left the law office and separated at the hotel. Bailey collected his rifle from his room, put it in the wagon waiting outside the general store, and went along to the stable for his horse. When he returned to the store Stella was sitting in the driving seat of the wagon and

Mike Pearson was lying on some straw in the back. Bailey tied his horse behind and climbed up to share the seat with Stella.

Cargill emerged from the store at that moment, carrying a box of shotgun cartridges. He waved as Stella cracked her whip. The team threw their weight against their harness and hauled the wagon out of Dodge in a cloud of dust, wheels grating. Bailey eased his pistol in its holster and held his Winchester in his left hand – just in case.

They left the township and followed the trail to the Pearson ranch. Bailey experienced a sense of relief as they hit the open range. Stella drove the team carefully, trying to ease the trip for her father. Bailey glanced over his shoulder at Mike Pearson and saw he was gripping a rifle and covering their backs. He looked to his front and settled down, hoping for a peaceful ride to the ranch. They did not converse. Stella was intent on picking the easiest going over the range and Bailey watched their surroundings, tense and ready for action.

They were in sight of the distant ranch when Mike Pearson shouted a warning. Bailey glanced over his shoulder and saw two riders pulling out of cover at the side of the trail about fifty yards behind them. They came at a gallop, gun smoke flaring around them. The crash of shots battered the silence and hurled harsh echoes across the range.

Stella whipped the team and the wagon jerked and rattled as the horses hit their top pace. Bailey glanced at her; saw that her face was pale, showing fear.

'Head for the ranch,' he shouted. 'We need cover.'

Mike Pearson's rifle cracked and echoes reverberated into the distance. Answering fire thudded into the woodwork of the wagon. Bailey twisted in his seat, braced himself, and fired at the pursuers. He didn't hit either man, but his shooting was accurate enough to force them back. They slackened speed and dropped out of range.

Stella shouted, and Bailey looked to his front. Stella had her hands full, busy with getting the best speed out of the horses. She jerked her head to the left. Bailey looked in that direction and saw riders appearing on a rise some 200 yards away.

'Henry Westcott is with them,' Stella cried. 'I recognize his horse.'

Bailey lifted his rifle to his shoulder. He swayed with the wagon and tried to centre his sights on Westcott's big figure, but the movement of the vehicle was against him. He fired, with no obvious effect, and lowered the rifle. He glanced at the ranch and reckoned they might not make it. Westcott's party was galloping now, sweeping in for the kill. Bailey levered a fresh cartridge into his rifle and waited, anxiously watching the decreasing distance between the wagon and the ranch. He saw that the riders were gaining on them, and would reach them while they were still out in the open.

'We're not going to make the ranch,' Bailey shouted. 'Be ready to stop the team when I tell you. I'm gonna have to fight them, and I'll have more chance if the wagon is still.'

Stella nodded. She whipped the team. The animals strained against their collars. The ranch drew perceptibly nearer. Bailey glanced over his shoulder, saw the two pursuers drawing closer again, and tension filled his mind. He checked his weapons and steeled himself for the coming fight. He had a brother to avenge, and needed not only the killer who had fired the fatal shot but everyone even remotely connected to the incident.

He looked ahead. The ranch was so near and yet too far. He saw a dip in the range fifty yards ahead.

'Stella, slow down when we hit that depression. I'll get out and unhitch my horse. But don't stop. Keep going to the ranch. OK?'

She glanced at him, tight-lipped, and nodded. He climbed over the seat and dropped into the body of the wagon. Mike Pearson was gripping his rifle, face taut, eyes showing what he was feeling. Bailey hurt his leg as he sprawled towards the rear of the wagon, and almost pitched over the back. He clung on with his right hand, leaned over the backboard and, after several attempts, managed to thrust his rifle into the saddle boot on his horse.

He unhitched his horse from the back of the wagon and hauled on his reins to pull the animal round to the side. Stella almost lost her seat as the wagon bounced into the long depression. She braced her legs and threw her weight backwards, pulling on the reins with all her strength. The horses slowed, and when she glanced over her shoulder she saw Bailey in the act of leaping on to the back of his horse. He made it and turned away. She returned her attention to driving and sent the team on again.

Bailey rode back to where the depression started, cursing the pain in his leg, and reined in. He dragged his rifle from its boot and sprang from the saddle. His injured leg refused to take his moving weight and he fell to the ground. Sweat ran down his face as he wormed his way up to the lip of the depression and looked around.

The two riders pursuing them from behind had gained ground. Bailey, breathing hard, hunkered down and lifted his rifle. His foresight wavered but he timed his shot and fired when the bead slid down from the head to the chest of the nearest rider. He shifted his aim as the man went out of his saddle, and aimed at the second man. As he fired again a bullet from one of the riders coming up from his left struck his left forearm. His rifle flew from his grasp. But he saw his second shot sweep his target from the saddle.

Blood spilled from his arm. He ignored it. Westcott and his riders were coming straight for him, surrounded by gun smoke, and slugs began thudding into the grass around him, raising dust spots. Bailey drew his pistol and began to shoot. His first slug sent Westcott back in his saddle. Westcott pulled on his reins and turned away, slowing his horse, and then fell sideways to the ground. Bailey shifted his aim and fired at the nearest of the six riders. The man fell out of his saddle. The others fanned out but kept coming. Bailey narrowed his eyes against gun smoke. He could feel pain raging in his right thigh, but his attention was centred on the men who wanted him dead. He ducked when a burst of concerted fire from the riders flailed the ground around him. He rolled over a couple of times and pushed himself up into a fresh aiming position.

The riders maintained a heavy fire. Bailey fired again, taking his time to aim at his target, and the rider fell forward over the neck of his horse before pitching to the ground. The other men changed direction and came in at an angle, separating as they pounded over the grass. Bailey changed position again, paused to snatch shells from his belt, and thumbed them into his cylinder.

An increase in the volume of fire filled him with a tightness that clawed at his throat. A rider came into the depression a few yards to his right, wheeled his mount, and then tried to halt, his gun hand moving swiftly to bring his gun to bear. Bailey shot him through the chest and then looked around. He could hear hoofs drumming just out of sight and held his fire. He pushed with his feet on the slope and stuck his head up out of the depression; was surprised to see that rest of his attackers had turned their horses away from him and were riding for cover. A second group of riders were in the background, urging their mounts forward, and gun smoke was drifting around them. He was delighted to see that he was not their target. They were shooting at Westcott's fleeing men.

But one of Westcott's riders was angling for the depression, and came fast to push his horse into its cover. He fired his pistol and Bailey felt the hammer-like blow of a striking bullet that sent him falling sideways. He tried desperately to get his sights lined up on the mounted man, fired and missed, and then fired again. The horse took the bullet in its chest and went down heavily, pushing its nose into the grass. It skidded towards Bailey while the rider tried to get Bailey in his sights. Bailey hurled himself to the left, rolled and then fired as his pistol came into line. The slug tore out the rider's throat. Blood spurted, and the man went out of his saddle.

Bailey could feel pain in his body. He sat up and looked for a wound. Blood was staining his shirt on his left hip. He felt as if he had been cut in half as he pushed to his feet, wanting to get to Stella. He hobbled to his waiting horse, ignoring the pain clawing at him, and hauled himself into the saddle. He rode out of the depression and sent the horse at a run for the ranch.

The wagon had halted in front of the ranch house and Stella was in the act of helping her father out of the vehicle. Bailey pushed the horse into making greater effort, and galloped into the yard as Stella and her father disappeared into the house. The sound of a shot came immediately from inside the building. Bailey hauled on his reins and skidded to a halt in front of the porch. He slid out of the saddle, and almost fell when he tried to walk. He tottered on to the porch, gun in hand, and lunged in through the doorway.

Mike Pearson was lying on the floor on the threshold and Stella was struggling in the grip of a man who was holding a pistol and trying to subdue her. She was grasping the gun wrist with both hands, trying to get the weapon from the man. Bailey blundered forward, trying desperately to maintain his balance. The man thrust Stella away and turned quickly, his gun hand lifting. Bailey moved instinctively, his pistol swinging up chest high. He saw the man's face and was shocked when he recognized Frank Hayman.

They fired simultaneously. Hayman's bullet missed Bailey by a hair's breadth. Bailey's slug thudded into Hayman's chest and he fell on his face. The sound of the shots seemed to go on for ever. Bailey staggered to a chair

157

and dropped into it. Stella got up and came to his side, exclaiming when she saw fresh blood on him.

'Hayman was in the house when we came in,' she said in a wavering tone. 'He said he had been waiting since yesterday for us to come back from Dodge. He was going to kill Dad and me and take over the ranch.'

'He killed my brother,' Bailey said, 'but he won't kill anyone else.'

The last echoes of the shooting drifted out of earshot and silence returned. Bailey sagged as his determination became exhausted but he did not care, for he suddenly realized that it was all over. He tried to hold on to his senses, his consciousness wavering, but he held on and his alertness returned. He suddenly realized that he was still holding his pistol, and checked it instinctively, refilling empty chambers.

'Is your father OK?' he demanded. 'I heard a shot as you entered the house.'

'Hayman pointed his gun at Dad and I pushed him off aim as he fired. It's a good thing you came with us. He would surely have killed us.'

Bailey's determination seeped away as pain increased its hold upon his body. The efforts of righting not only his personal wrongs but bringing justice to the bad-men in Dodge City had exhausted him and he gave up the struggle. He looked up into Stella's face, saw grave concern etched into every line of her countenance, and realized that she no longer seemed like a stranger. He closed his eyes wearily and plunged into the dark pit of unconsciousness that enveloped him, but not before his mind had seized on a single stark truth – his future was not in

California but here, where Fate had crossed his trail with that of Stella Pearson, and he clung to the hope that Fate had not yet done with him.

Stella, worriedly assessing his wounds, was surprised to see a smile appear on his lips.